Julie Bozza

The Fine Point of His Soul

LIBRAtiger

Published by LIBRAtiger

ISBN: 978-0-9955465-0-9

First published: 2012
Revised edition: 2016

Text: © Julie Bozza 2016
Editing and proofreading: Two Marshmallows | twomarshmallows.net
Book format: © Julie Bozza 2016
Set in Adobe Caslon and Pristina

Cover image: © bpk Bildagentur für Kunst, Kultur und Geschichte, Berlin | from the Kurfürstlichen Galerie Schleißheim | location Bayerische Staatsgemäldesammlungen, Alte Pinakothek München | attributed to Giorgione da Castelfranco, *Brustbild einen jungen Mannes* (Half-length portrait of a young man)
Cover design: © Michelle Peart 2016

libra–tiger.com | juliebozza.com

Dedication

To my sister, without whom…

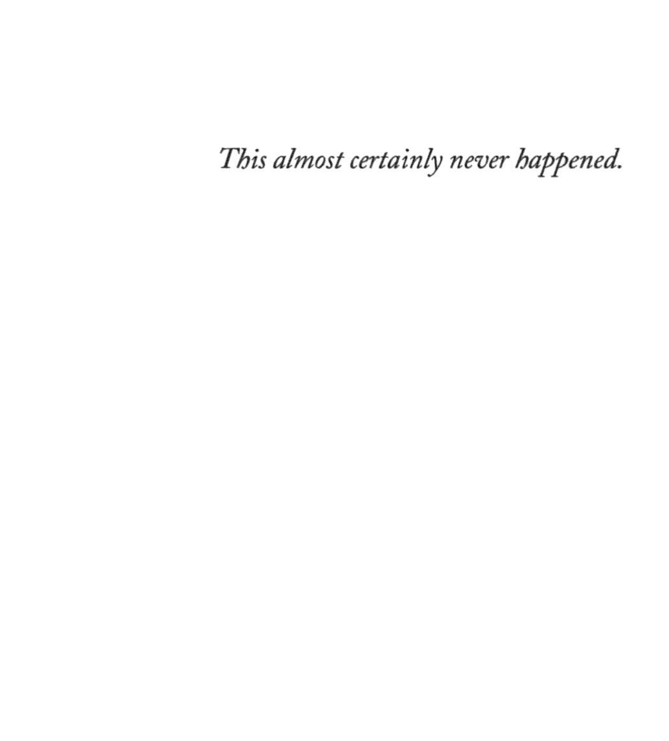

This almost certainly never happened.

Contents

'Her immortal part with angels lives…'

She was laid out in her wedding clothes, a modest ensemble first worn seven years before. My eyes dwelt long on the worn bible in her hands and the scattered silk lilies, for I dreaded my last sight of her beautiful face. When I finally lifted my gaze I was near undone.

There are times when death brings serenity to a person; I had seen this often enough even in the midst of war, and I always gave thanks for such grace. It was not so now. Her face, which I remembered in shared laughter, which had radiated a profound kind of contentment – her face was now troubled and drawn. She had died but the day before, and the undertaker's best arts had been applied, and yet she did not seem tranquil.

She was gone. Peace was destroyed.

Seven Souls Heavy – October 1820

His Majesty's Ship *Boadicea* dropped anchor amidst a mass of ships in the Bay of Naples. We'd been far too long from home and were desperate for news, so we were delighted to hear from one of the local merchants that the brig *Maria Crowther* was lately arrived from England, and was anchored about half a nautical mile from us. The querying look I cast my captain was hardly needed. "Lieutenant Sullivan," he called in response, "take a boat over, and offer my compliments."

I picked the six nearest men to accompany me, and others were already readying a boat to be lowered. The swarm of merchants and other hopefuls plying their trades from various watercraft made way for us, and cheerfully took the opportunity to importune us as we passed.

The men rowed with vigour, as I steered us through the crowd of ships. I had no direct sight of the brig for most of the journey, but had plotted our course while still on board the *Boadicea* with a view of the intervening anchorages. The Bay was so full that I thought there must be as many people on the sea as on land.

Soon we were alongside the *Maria Crowther*. A gathering of dismayed faces peered down at us from the deck, but I gave this no thought, even when one of my men queried uncertainly, "Sir...?"

A Jacob's ladder hung down the side of the brig, so I leapt onto it and ran up, crying, "What news from Mother England?"

Amidst the dismayed faces, one young man was bubbling irresistibly into laughter. Everyone else was shocked immobile yet the young man was full of ironic merriment. "Oh, the worst, the worst," he replied, though the tears he wiped from his eyes were not springing from grief.

A babble from the others soon had me completely taken aback. "Quarantine, sir," said an older man, who I took from his authoritative bearing to be the captain. "We are in *quarantine*." It seemed there had been an outbreak of typhus in England, and the authorities in Naples were being overly cautious.

"Welcome to Purgatory," the young man intoned. He'd had his hand on his heart, but when he saw me staring at him, he offered a salute half polite and half merry.

And it was too late. I turned, and could already see the harbourmaster's boat approaching to order us confined, and a crowded ship became seven unwelcome souls heavier.

My six men helped the brig's crew cheerfully enough, or kept to themselves as much as they could on an eighty-foot boat carrying eighteen people. They were good men and never said a word about my poor judgement, though they could hardly be happy about this confinement. Meanwhile I tried to make myself as pleasant a companion as circumstances permitted.

The young man who had so enjoyed the irony of my precipitate arrival was named John Keats, one of four passengers on the brig which had sailed from London over a month before. Keats had a well-proportioned compact form, strong handsome features, and thick reddish-brown curls. Despite his energy and good-humoured engagement with all around him, it was soon obvious that he was severely ill.

"I am to winter in Rome," he explained, "where the dry classical air is to heal me." Catching his friend's fretful glance, Keats added, "Alternatively, I may join the ancients resting in that eternal city – but I do not intend to do so until I am quite hoary myself."

I introduced myself: "Sullivan. Lieutenant Andrew Sullivan of the frigate *Boadicea*."

"Joseph Severn," Keats' friend said in turn, shaking my hand. Severn had little of Keats' confident manner. He was slim and seemed forever uncertain, with a narrow face hidden amidst overly long brown curls.

"Severn is an artist," Keats provided when his friend did not. "The Royal Academy awarded him a Gold Medal for his last work – a prize they have not seen fit to award for twelve years. He seeks subject matter for future glories in Rome!"

"Indeed, I do paint," Severn supplied with a blush, "but that is nothing. Keats here is a poet, and his words will be stirring hearts for decades after my works have turned to dust and are forgotten."

"Ah! I will outdo you in modesty, as I swear your *Cave of Despair* will hang with the most revered works for centuries."

"Now, do not be foolish," his friend chided Keats sincerely. "You know full well I will be forgotten, while through the ages you will rank second only to Shakespeare."

"Shakespeare!" I cried in surprise. They both looked at me with silent enquiry. "What know you of Shakespeare?"

"A little," said Keats.

"He is being modest again," Severn supplied.

"And his plays? *Othello, the Moor of Venice*, for instance? Or…" I racked my memory. "Or *Hamlet, Prince of Denmark*?"

"Yes." And he waited with a raised brow, obviously wondering what my sudden interest could mean.

But these seemingly small innocuous matters may have led me into deep and turbulent waters. I judged it better to retreat for now. "Then perhaps we will speak of them by and by."

Keats nodded. "I have a copy of Shakespeare's *Works* with me," he said, before tactfully redirecting the conversation. "What do you read, Lieutenant? You are required to be expert in mathematics, I suppose."

"I try to study geometry as thoroughly as I may, which is essential for navigation, and I have some interest in natural philosophy."

"Of course!" And we spoke for a while of that, and of the beautiful Bay of Naples, and of Mount Vesuvius which loomed over us with its ever-present columns of smoke turning amber and then gold in the sunlight. We spoke of anything, in fact, but Shakespeare and *Othello*. Yet I could think of little else.

The other two passengers were women, one of whom – a Miss Cotterell – was evidently even more poorly than Keats. It was soon clear she was consumptive; tragic in a pretty creature not yet twenty. She would be so racked with coughs that she fainted, and Keats and Severn would take care of her as best they might. I discovered that Keats had some medical training himself, and had qualified as an apothecary.

One afternoon, once Miss Cotterell was settled quietly in the cabin again, Keats came back out on deck with a bitter set to his mouth. It can't have been pleasant to be so intimately reminded of his mortality. He coughed a little in the brisk air, and I thought I spied drops of blood on his handkerchief before he pushed it back into his trouser pocket. He took something small and white from his other pocket and toyed with it for a few moments before returning it home.

I wandered over to him as he sat down and picked up the volume he'd been browsing. It was his Shakespeare, of course. I wondered if he'd been reading *Othello*. He smiled politely when he saw I'd noticed the book, and left a pause, but when I didn't introduce the topic he spoke of something else. "I had no idea the Bay was so vast," Keats said, "nor that it could contain so very many ships. How many do you think there are?"

"Perhaps fifty boats in the local fishing fleet," I hazarded. "Maybe twenty times that number in ships of all kinds."

Keats shook his head, and looked about him once more. "A bristling thicket of masts. Cobwebs of rigging. And here we are, trapped in the midst of it all. But if we're the prey, who's the spider?"

I laughed at his fancies. Then I asked, "Did you know that it's only the spiral threads of a cobweb that are sticky? The radiating threads are not – and they're what the spider must use, else trap itself."

"Is that so?" he asked with an interested gleam in his eye. But my fund of natural philosophy didn't hold his interest for long. Soon enough he was gazing at the sandy-coloured stone of the old fort, then the jumbled rooftops and spires rising up the foothills, and beyond them the vineyards climbing steeper still. Keats sighed. "One wishes for an end to it all, an end to the struggles – whether one succeeds by breaking free or by attracting the attention of the spider."

At least we were well-provisioned in our web, for the harbourmaster did not seem to care who drew their boats up alongside the *Maria Crowther*, just so long as none of us left the ship and no one else boarded her. The crew had devised a system of ropes and pulleys to raise the goods up the side and lower any payments required, any mail to be dispatched.

My captain sent supplies, more than enough for all eighteen. Miss Cotterell's brother Charles, a banker in Naples, had all manner of treats brought out. And then night and day the local merchants rowed from ship to ship, selling fresh food and trinkets, exchanging banter and gossip. The two women bought colourful woven shawls and my men endeavoured to outdo them with brightly patterned neckerchiefs.

We all tried to make the wait bearable. And yet we seasoned men were as giddy with relief as Miss Cotterell was when the quarantine was finally lifted on the last day of October.

I accompanied Keats and Severn ashore, and saw them settled into lodgings in the Guanti Nuovi district. And then my six men and I returned to the *Boadicea*. The whole party had split apart within an hour or two of the end of our confinement. I'm sure most of us had no desire to ever set eyes on the others again. And yet it was my fate to become intimately acquainted with John Keats during the next few months.

My Captain's Request – November 1820

I took two visitors with me to see Keats the next morning. "May I introduce Captain Sir William Mitchell of the *Boadicea*, and our ship's surgeon, Mr Geraint Bannon."

"A great pleasure to make your acquaintance," Keats said, shaking their hands in turn. He seemed to be caught a little off-guard, though he hid it well, and he was soon genuinely engaging in conversation. Severn, on the other hand, barely spoke; I knew already that he would retreat into shyness when flummoxed. "We must thank you again, Captain, for your generosity in supplying our ship during the unfortunate quarantine."

"The least we could do after Sullivan here blundered aboard. We must apologise again for the inconvenience he and the men caused."

"Not at all!" Keats cried. "The Lieutenant was the most amiable of companions, and I do believe the men worked so hard on the ship they were soon considered more a convenience than otherwise."

"Excellent, excellent," Mitchell responded. Then he glanced at me and at Bannon, and said, "But our time here must be short."

Bannon cleared his throat, and with a tilt of his head invited Keats to step aside. "Forgive the impertinence, Mr Keats," he said in a low voice that I could nevertheless hear. "I understand from Lieutenant Sullivan that you have come to Italy for your health."

Keats confirmed this, and soon the two were conferring quietly with heads together, with utter dispassion as if they were discussing a third party. I heard enough to gather there was some doubt as to whether Keats' heart, stomach or lungs were the most likely cause of his illness. I did not think it could be his heart.

The Captain and I tried to converse with Severn on art and on Italy, but we hadn't made much headway before Mitchell spied Keats' stacked volumes of Shakespeare; he soon had his nose buried amidst the pages. Severn and I managed to occupy ourselves with talk of visas and passports and the best road to Rome.

"I greatly appreciate your advice," Keats said as he and Bannon finally rejoined us. "It is contrary to some, but it accords with my own instincts."

"Then I wish you better health in the days to come." They shook hands.

Keats looked around, about to address us all, but then he paused as he felt our expectant silence. A moment passed.

"This Iago fellow," Captain Mitchell precipitately began, indicating the book he held. "What can you tell me of him?"

"A villain," Keats promptly responded. "Perhaps the most sinister in all of Shakespeare's plays, for he deceives everyone into thinking him honest and wholly reliable."

"But he destroys them all, doesn't he? Othello's wife, his own wife, and Othello himself…"

"Yes, and Desdemona was innocent, while Othello was guilty of little more than jealousy."

"*Why* does he do it?"

Keats took a breath. "There is much discussion on that very question. No one agrees." But he saw that such an answer would not do. "Iago declares that he resents being passed over for promotion; that is supposedly his main motive. Though as you'd know, Othello is a Moor, and Iago refers to him with disgust as a *black ram*; that might add to his reasons. He also says he suspects that Othello might have betrayed Iago with his wife Emilia." Keats gestured expansively. "It could be all these things or none of them."

Mitchell sighed, and did not respond. His eyes drifted back to the book, and he turned a page or two as if looking for answers there.

"May I ask," Keats said carefully, "why you are interested? It might help me find something of use to you."

I didn't think Mitchell would tell him anything of the matter. But he glanced at me, as if asking again whether Keats was to be trusted; I nodded once firmly. And then my captain said in a rough voice, "My wife… My wife's brother has stolen something from me. And now I understand he is in Rome. I… I hear he is calling himself Iago."

Keats frowned. Severn could not hide his astonishment.

"And so I seek to fathom his reasons… If indeed he has any," Mitchell added bitterly.

"I see," said Keats slowly. "Well, if you would let me read the play again this evening, and mull it over…"

"We have little time." Even as Mitchell spoke, his gaze darted down towards the street, and we all heard a carriage approaching at speed. "Sullivan goes to Rome on my behalf," Mitchell said with urgency. "Mr

Keats, you would do me a great favour if you'd permit him to travel with you and Mr Severn as your companion."

"Of course," Keats immediately said, though he was almost as astonished as Severn by now.

"A greater favour still, if you would advise him in any way you can on this villain."

"Yes. Yes, of course," Keats reassured him. "But do you not –?"

"Captain Mitchell!" bellowed a voice from below. "Captain Mitchell, are you in there, sir?"

We heard at least three sets of feet pounding up the stairs, and the clatter of weaponry. Severn looked bewildered and terrified. Keats was obviously surprised, but stood firm. The Captain glanced at me, and I nodded my understanding; I quickly stepped further back in the room, so that I stood aligned with Keats and Severn rather than with Mitchell and Bannon.

They had the courtesy to knock on the door, though they did not wait for an invitation before pushing it open. Severn shrank back to the wall. "It is the British Consul," I murmured to him and Keats. He had brought two soldiers.

"*You*, sir," the Consul spluttered, pointing a damning finger at Captain Mitchell, "were under oath not to set foot ashore. Explain yourself, sir!"

"A social visit," Mitchell said with a calm shrug. He indicated Keats. "A cousin of my dearest friend. I wanted news of him."

The Consul was shaking his head, determined not to believe a word of it. "You could have had him brought to the *Boadicea*."

Keats gave a sincere shudder. "I have had enough of boats to last me a lifetime."

A dismissive stare from the Consul swept over Keats and returned to Mitchell. "You will return to your ship *now*, sir."

Mitchell cocked an eyebrow at him, yet said peaceably, "As you wish." He nodded farewell at the three of us. "Gentlemen." Then he swept out, with Bannon right behind him. The Consul glared at us, and then followed them out, bawling at the solders to accompany Mitchell and Bannon to the docks and see them afloat.

After a few minutes, peace returned. Keats went to Severn, examined his expression, and then grasped his shoulder reassuringly. "All right, dearheart?"

"Yes." Though Severn went to sit down, and it seemed his hands were shaking.

Keats looked at me next. "I don't entirely understand…"

"I don't have the full story myself. Some of the particulars relate to Captain Mitchell's family, and some to state matters."

"*State* matters?"

I nodded confirmation, hardly trusting myself to know what best to divulge. Yet my captain had himself involved Keats in this.

"Then I take it the Captain has heard of his brother-in-law's doings through his wife, but also through other channels? Naval? Diplomatic?"

"The Captain's wife is dead."

"I am sorry," Keats murmured. He sighed and turned away. "It is a strange thing, to take on such a name… But I will re-read the play. Perhaps it will give us some clue."

"Perhaps," I said. I didn't hold much hope.

For a moment we were all stranded in a contemplative silence. But then Keats clapped his hands together as if to awaken us, and declared, "Well, I for one want a hearty meal."

Severn looked at him worriedly. "Are you sure that –"

"It is my new medical regime, on advice from Mr Bannon," Keats briskly replied. He seemed rather pleased about it.

"John, I know you are trained and know far more of this than I do, but you promised me you would heed the best advice of others."

"And so I am. Let's go and eat like *men*."

The three of us applied for both British and Papal visas, and were advised they would take a week or more to be approved. To try to avoid any embarrassment for Captain Mitchell, I applied as Mr Sullivan: no longer an officer, but still a gentleman. Also, I stated that I was a carpenter, which was after all the trade I had been in before I was pressed into service.

Charles Cotterell helped occupy our days with tours of vineyards and extravagant churches and the ruins of Pompeii. We also attended my first and no doubt my last opera. Keats started helping me through it with murmured explanations of the plot and of the more unexpected traits of such productions, until he realised that the soldiers posted by the stage weren't part of the cast or scenic decorations. After that he was too angry to enjoy the rest of the performance, and his mutterings were now only complaints at the idea of them being there to suppress the populace, a visible token of a tyrannous regime.

On the following day, one of the midshipmen brought my belongings and dress uniform ashore, neatly stowed in a newly sewn canvas bag. We met at one of the dockside taverns, where we might go unnoticed or at least remain anonymous. Such precautions were perhaps unnecessary, but I would have hated to fail my captain by being discovered and sent back to the *Boadicea* with nothing to show for our trouble. Of course the midshipman tried to quiz me on what I was doing ashore, but I repelled his curiosity with talk of possible new supplies of wood and other gear. I don't think he believed me, but it did at least dampen his conversation.

There were long afternoons when a constant drizzle of rain made outings inadvisable for Keats and unpleasant for Severn and me. Keats would sit and read quietly, whether novels or plays, poetry or histories; so lost in the words he hardly moved for hours at a stretch. Often he would take the small white object from his pocket, and absently play with it in one hand. I finally saw that it was a small stone, almost spherical and highly polished, with a few transparent lines running through the opaque frozen milkiness. It seemed precious to him; occasionally he would hold it in his fisted hand against his heart.

Meanwhile Severn would sketch the view from the window or from his imagination, or he would draw Keats' profile again and again, trying to complete it in one perfect line. I read, too, though I was little in the mood for the geometry tome my captain had sent me in that new canvas bag, and Shakespeare's versifying felt beyond me. Instead, I borrowed tools from the neighbours, and fixed two of the chairs in our lodgings. When I found an odd block of wood, a discarded off-cut, I began carving, uncovering a strong-featured face with thick curly hair.

A letter came for Keats one morning. He read it through thoughtfully, and then took it to Severn before wandering across to the window with his hands stuffed deep in his pockets. "Shelley again," Keats announced to his friend. "He suggests we go to him in Pisa."

Severn's eyes darted over it back and forth and back again, before he responded with a discontented frown. "He does not offer you the same hospitality as he did in his last."

Keats shrugged. "He would take us in if he found us on his doorstep."

"I should hope so!"

"His last letter was the quintessence of generosity, and only *mildly* condescending." He smiled mischievously. "Really, it was beneath me to even notice."

"Who is Shelley?" I asked.

"A poet," Keats replied. "*Queen Mab. Alastor. The Revolt of Islam.*"

"The eldest son of a baronet," Severn supplied.

"In any event," Keats said with a nod to me, "we are committed to Rome now."

"Captain Mitchell asked only that I travel with you," I said. "Though if you have any advice on the issue of the name Iago, I would appreciate it."

He shook his head. "I'm not coming up with anything more than the obvious: The man intends irony, humour or harm. I don't know that I can be much use to you in Rome."

Severn said fretfully, "The weather in Rome is no doubt warmer and drier. It is so much further south than Pisa! And further inland, too, I believe. The warmer climate was the whole object of our disastrous voyage, was it not?"

"Of course, my friend," Keats gently confirmed with a smile. "Well, Andrew, we will see you settled in Rome, at least, and take a look around ourselves. And then we will decide."

Eventually the passports were ready for collection. We said our farewells to Cotterell, hired a carriage, and set off along the old Appian Way. It was the eighth of November, and it would take us until the fifteenth to reach Rome.

It was a tedious journey through an impoverished countryside. I was used to the meagre comforts of life aboard ship, and had considered our shared lodgings in Naples a pleasant and refreshing change, but the dirt and squalor we now faced each evening disheartened even me. The pity of it was that this was how the people here lived, day in and day out.

"I would rather be back in our cabin on board the *Maria Crowther*," Severn muttered at the end of our second day.

Keats shuddered, and pointed out, "This room is not three foot deep in brine."

"True."

"And there is no Miss Cotterell to wake us with her hacking coughs… Well, though," Keats added after a moment, with a shamed look on his face, "you still have to put up with mine."

Severn was gazing at him anxiously. "You have been better, I swear it. You've hardly coughed at all these past few nights. Is that not so, Sullivan?"

"You have been better," I affirmed, though I could sleep through anything – a necessary survival trait on a ship – and Keats had never woken me. But during the days he seemed brighter and more comfortable in himself, and was slowly gaining in energy.

"There, you see," Keats said to Severn. "Mr Bannon's advice is bearing fruit."

But Severn was still sceptical. "We will consult with Dr Clark in Rome. You'll recall he is a specialist in this field."

"All right, dearheart." Keats smiled as he watched Severn set about making the room as presentable as possible.

It was obvious that Keats was very fond of Severn though the man was timid and liked everything to be *just so,* which of course it never was and never could be. Severn seemed far younger than Keats, though Severn was almost twenty-seven, while Keats had just turned twenty-five, my own age. And yet Severn had been brave enough to accompany his friend to Italy, committing himself to nurse Keats through a potentially desperate illness, despite a very real chance that Keats might die and leave him there alone to cope with his grief and all the mundane practicalities. For that he deserved to be honoured.

The next day I walked alongside the carriage for much of the way, as had become my habit. It gave me exercise, saved me from the constant jolting of the uneven roads, and it allowed the others more room and comfort. Severn would occasionally join me for a while.

He did so when we reached a long plain of grasslands brightened with wildflowers. The prospect delighted us all. To share it with his friend, Severn strode far and wide gathering armfuls of colour, and then he ran back and tossed them through the carriage window to lie at the poet's feet. Keats laughed happily, and watched his friend with true affection. In that moment I even began to warm towards Severn myself.

The approach to Rome itself was less happy. Along each side of the Appian Way were displayed the bodies of executed criminals in various stages of decay. Our hearts had lifted at the thought of our journey at last ending, but now Severn blanched and shrank back into the darkest corner of the carriage. Even the usually steady Keats seemed horrified by this reminder of the fate that awaited him. He pushed his hand into his pocket and clutched at the white stone for comfort, apparently without being conscious of the action. Death threatens us all, of course, but some it presses closer than others.

"The city itself will be bursting with life," I offered. "All will be different once we pass through the walls."

"Perhaps," said Keats.

"Come, Severn, think about the lodgings we will have tonight. They will seem fit for a king after what we have endured this past week."

Severn did little more than nod in acknowledgement of my efforts, but soon enough he was visibly thinking and planning, and paid no more attention to the grim parade beyond the carriage windows.

The First Day

Eventually our carriage clattered into the Piazza di Spagna and we disembarked, stretching our weary bones. The piazza was long and narrow, an irregular shape. We were near a fountain in which a half-sunken boat burbled water over its sides: the most peaceful shipwreck I ever saw or heard. A wide flight of steps led steeply to an old church with two square towers. And it was all crowded. There were flower sellers throughout the piazza, a busy stables off to one side, the Spanish Embassy of course, a coffee house, a trattoria, and parties interested in all these and in each other. Mingling on the marble stairway were a bewildering variety of people in picturesque costumes. Severn later explained that they would hire out as artists' models; for now he just seemed bemused by it all.

Keats, on the other hand, looked around with a growing grin of satisfaction. "This is more like it!" he cried, clapping his hands together. "*This* is the Italy I have longed for."

I had to agree with him. The sunshine helped, and Keats' delight was infectious.

"I will find Dr Clark," said Severn.

While Severn bustled off, I stayed with the carriage and our baggage, and Keats wandered across to the fountain and back, gazing around him with appreciation. The murmur of the crowd rose and fell in waves around us, occasionally drowning out the constant fountain.

Keats turned his face to the sunlight, his eyes closed as he drank in the warmth. "Apollo is blessing us."

"Apollo?"

"The sun god of the Greeks and the Romans. And my own god, for he is the god of both poetry and healing." Then he looked directly at me, and winked, as if to assuage any shock I might feel over him breaking the first commandment.

"Here they are," Severn announced, calling our attention to his companion. He introduced us to Dr James Clark, a distinguished though approachable-looking fellow in his early thirties.

The doctor greeted me kindly in a soft Scottish burr, but of course his attention was focused on Keats; his gaze seemed to analyse Keats' condition in one long sweep. Keats bore the examination bravely, and certainly seemed bright enough. However, I was disheartened to glimpse a troubled look in Clark's eyes as he turned back to include Severn and me. "Well," Clark said, "I have been expecting you for some time now."

"We left England on the seventeenth of September," said a bitter Severn. Fifty-nine days before. "It has been a truly hellish journey."

"I'll warrant it has. So, let's end that journey rather than idle here in pleasantries; I'm sure you're keen to settle now you're here at last. I'll show you the lodgings I've secured for you. Though," Clark added, casting a doubtful glance in my direction, "I had not thought there would be three of you."

"Never mind me, Dr Clark," I said. "I'll carry the cases up for you, and then make my own arrangements."

"You will not!" Keats protested. Then he took a breath, and offered politely, "You're welcome to stay with us, though of course you'd probably be more comfortable elsewhere."

Severn was looking at me a bit anxiously, and I flattered myself that he and Keats had already come to rely on me to some small extent. It was also true that I already valued Keats' friendship highly. "Let's decide that tomorrow, then," I offered as a compromise. "As long as there's a length of floor I can stretch out on for tonight, I'll be happy."

Clark tilted his head to pointedly measure my height; I was by far the tallest of the four of us. "Well, perhaps you might just fit," he murmured, "lying diagonally across the sitting room." Then he winked at me, and led the way to a house at the very foot of the great stairway.

The lodgings were on the second floor, with three rooms making an L shape. The sitting room was a decent size, running along the front of the building. The corner room, looking out over both the piazza and the stairway, would be Keats' bedroom; Severn and I agreed that between us with a glance. From there a door opened onto a small square room.

Severn examined this doubtfully. "I'd been hoping to have a room for my painting…"

"Then if this will suit, you and I will make up beds in the sitting room," I suggested. "I'm honestly happy with the floor, if you'll take the sofa."

He smiled at me. "Thank you, Lieutenant Sullivan."

I grimaced. "*Mr* Sullivan for any new acquaintance in Rome, but as my friend you must call me Andrew."

Severn's smile grew, acknowledging that we had at last reached some kind of understanding. "And you will call me Joseph."

Then a moment later he was off to organise the unpacking and rearrange the furniture in ways that accorded with his views on what was good and right.

Back in the sitting room, I found Clark and Keats in an earnest conversation about medical matters. It seemed that despite the whispers there was a disagreement or even an argument growing. I would have retreated but Keats himself stepped away from Clark, and beckoned me in. "You and Severn have got us shipshape already?" he asked.

"Not quite," I replied with a smile, "but we're on the way." A tuneless industrious humming could be heard from the bedroom.

"Excellent."

"Well," said a discomfited Clark, "I'll let you get settled. Mr Keats, I trust we'll talk again tomorrow."

"Of course. Thank you for all your efforts, Dr Clark. The lodgings will suit us perfectly." They shook hands, and then Clark left with a farewell nod to me.

Keats stood utterly still for a moment, lost in contemplation, but when he finally turned to me he had a fiery look in his eye. "Andrew, whatever happens, *don't let him bleed me.* You understand? It was your own Mr Bannon who first said as much, but I agreed with all my heart. Dr Clark will insist, and Severn would let himself be overruled, so you must stand by me on this."

This took me aback. Eventually I said enough to indicate that I understood bleeding to be an unpleasant but necessary and generally accepted practice.

Keats nodded. "It goes against my own medical training to refuse it, and yet that's what all my instincts clamour for me to do." He turned away a little, as if needing the space to consider whether to continue. Then he said in a low voice, "My own brother, my youngest brother Tom, poor soul… I took care of him as he died of consumption. The bleeding weakened him. It is supposed to purge you of bad humours, or reduce an overabundance of blood. But Mr Bannon suggested that it does more harm than good in most cases, and I concur."

"Can you assure me that it did not help your brother? Would you swear it?"

It seemed that after all he was not sure, or perhaps he was afraid of the honest answer, for Keats eventually replied, "It was not for me to experiment with Tom's life. But I must be allowed the dignity of deciding what to do with my own."

And to this I assented.

The trattoria directly opposite our lodgings sent us dinner, which we ate in our sitting room, and then I took a turn around the piazza. Though it was quite late and the night was dark, the air was cool rather than cold. It seemed dry, which I supposed was why people such as Keats left the damp climate of England; but it was too dry for me, and I missed the salty tang of the ocean.

When I returned to our rooms, I found Severn writing a letter at the only table. Keats was on the sofa with his feet up on a chair, and he held a book in his lap but was gazing off distractedly as if his focus was far distant. I grabbed the nearest book – various volumes were already scattered throughout the room – and settled on the other end of the sofa.

"How will we know him?"

I glanced up, and found Keats looking at me expectantly. Severn shifted around in his chair to await my response. "I beg your pardon?"

"How will we know this Iago fellow?"

"Ah." I sat forward, leaning my elbows on my knees, again wondering how much to tell them of what little I knew. "I understand he has leased the Palazzo Amara on the Corso."

Severn frowned at this, as if the place meant something to him.

"And there is this…" I reached for the small pouch that I wore round my neck hung on a leather thong. Captain Mitchell had required that I guard this with all but my life.

Severn drew closer and they both watched me as I carefully took my captain's last remaining treasure from the pouch, and unwrapped first a layer of canvas and then of silk. The treasure was a locket, a large gold oval with a delicate tracery of leaves around the lower edge. I carefully depressed the catch, and looked at the two miniatures within for a moment before passing it over. Keats received it with suitable care, and they both bent their heads over it.

"That is Mrs Mitchell, from before she was married."

"She was very beautiful," Keats murmured.

"Yes. The Captain said this likeness was taken ten years ago or more. Naturally she had… matured since then, but it only improved her." If I closed my eyes I could still conjure a vision of her from the dinner she'd hosted for all her husband's officers before we set sail in mid-summer. She'd had a round, friendly, candid face, with a surprisingly engaging smile. Thick red curls framed ivory skin and dark brown eyes. She always seemed to be having fun even on the most ordinary occasions. I had envied my captain his luck.

"And so this –"

"Yes. The other is her brother, taken at the same time. He was a decade older than her. The locket belonged to their father, and he left it to Captain Mitchell when he died." I wondered if I was seeing only what I looked to find in her brother's portrait, for I had never met him and could not compare the image with the person himself. But it seemed to me that the siblings were similar in almost every respect, with only these exceptions: his features were stronger and very masculine; his expression was reserved rather than candid; and his eyes were the strangest light green.

"What is his name?" Keats eventually asked. "His true name?"

"Hart," I told them. "Adrian Hart. And Mrs Mitchell's name was Lady Elena."

Giddiness and Bitterness

"Palazzo Amara!" Severn cried the next morning, rushing into the sitting room brandishing a letter. "I knew I recognised the name. It is one of the places I have an introduction for."

Keats raised a brow. I must have looked astonished. "You have a letter of introduction for Hart?"

"No, no, no. It is for the artwork there; a fine collection of old masters. My tutor at the Academy recommended I visit, and he gave me this to vouchsafe my credentials. I have a few such, for various places."

My own origins were humble, and I had to admit to being a little out of my depth. "Would it enable us to meet him?" I asked – though even as I said it, I wondered whether that would be a wise course of action.

"Well, no." Severn looked rather self-conscious as he explained. "It would be enough for the housekeeper to let me in and show me round the gallery. Nothing more than that."

I nodded, considering this. It seemed like a marvellous opportunity that we must make the most of. But it wouldn't do to rush in without any plan or firm intention.

Keats seemed to agree. "First I think we need to do some research."

"Yes."

"How do people know him, what do they call him? What is his stated purpose for being here? What do people think he's up to, if anything?"

I smiled as I looked at Keats. He seemed intrigued, and it made his eyes glint like the sun off the ocean.

We began with Dr Clark when he arrived soon after breakfast. Keats submitted to his attentions for a short period, while Severn and I withdrew to the other room. Severn busied himself by making up Keats' bed. I stood at the window and distracted myself by silently noting all the points on which the sunken boat in the fountain departed from reality; there were many.

Soon enough, Keats called us back through.

"How is he, sir?" Severn asked.

Clark seemed a little puzzled. "Perhaps better for a good night's rest."

"They have been few enough of late," I confirmed.

"Dr Clark," Keats said, "do you know of an Englishman, a Mr Adrian Hart, who has taken the Palazzo Amara on the Corso? That's not far from here, is it?"

Clark looked from one to the other of us, his puzzlement growing. "Well, I confess I have heard such a man mentioned. I never heard his name. There have been some oddities – no doubt it is nothing more than gossip, however…"

"What oddities?"

"He has created a bit of a stir, I think. He is… intriguing."

When no details were forthcoming, I asked outright. "I have heard he was calling himself by the name of one of Shakespeare's villains. Is that so?"

But Clark was getting warier by the moment. He looked round at each of us once more. "Why do you ask? What is this man to you?"

I shook my head. Severn seemed struck mute. Keats sat back and offered, "Oh, I'm sure it's just gossip, as you say, Dr Clark. We heard he was going by the name Iago, and we were indeed intrigued."

"Well, I suspect he is not the sort of man to be patient with the curious," Clark said in tones indicating that he trusted he had now heard the end of it. He paused for a moment, but when none of us pursued the matter he continued, "I have advised Mr Keats that some light exercise would be beneficial. The Pincian Hill is a stroll away. Perhaps you gentlemen would undertake to accompany him there each day."

"Of course," I promised.

"Yes, of course," echoed Severn. He politely saw Dr Clark out.

When the three of us were gathered together again, Keats grinned and added, "Of course. The Pincian Hill. Daily. And we can return along the Corso."

We all three chuckled like naughty schoolboys.

Marble stairways wound to and fro up the Pincian Hill, and then pathways led through the parklands and formal gardens. All manner of statues were placed at every junction. People of society strolled along, watching each other and displaying themselves. Lowlier types like us took the air, enjoying the autumnal warmth. If it wasn't for the task I must pursue, I would have enjoyed it greatly.

My captain had involved Keats in this, and I liked him on his own account, so I was committed to helping Severn take care of him. And yet I must not forget where my priorities lay.

Soon enough we were wandering back towards the Piazza di Spagna, though approaching it from a north-westerly angle. We crossed the wide open Piazza del Popolo, passing the Egyptian obelisk at its centre, and entered the Via del Corso. Severn was giddy with daring, while Keats was quietly afire with excitement but also amused at himself and his friend. I caught a little of all these moods from them – though surely all we would see was the frontage of a palazzo that anybody with enough funds might have leased.

The palazzo showed an impressively ornate façade to the world. Pristine white marble soared three stories high. No edge was left unadorned by carving or statuary, except for a final clean curve aglow with sunlight against the deep blue sky. A broad set of steps swept up to a double front door that must be fifteen foot tall. It seemed that no one was about; I felt as if the palazzo were closed for now but not abandoned. The three of us strolled past, gaping like a fresh batch of tourists – which I suppose we were. Then we were beyond the marble, and instead a wall of honey-coloured stone apparently enclosed the palazzo's garden.

And then it was over, and we were back in the mundane world of the Corso. High class shops and hotels lined the street, while a bustle of high class people surrounded us. We strolled down to the Via Condotti which would take us back to the Piazza di Spagna. This circuit would become our daily walk, and as it was an unexceptional route for visitors to Rome it attracted no comment.

"No doubt you will want to find yourself more comfortable quarters," Keats suggested to me as we sat in the sitting room on our second evening in Rome. "Though I hope for our sake you will remain nearby."

I considered this, although I already knew what I wanted to do. My captain had given me ample funds, but had also advised me to maintain as discreet a lifestyle as possible. It would be no hardship to remain here as Keats' companion along with Severn. And I already suspected, though for no good reason, that Keats may well play a part in this task I'd been set. "I'd like to stay here," I said, "if I am not too large a burden."

"The floor cannot make a decent bed," Severn observed.

"No, but I could find myself a bedroll and be perfectly content."

Keats smiled a little. "I suppose a sailor daily faces hardships worse than the lack of a feather bed."

"I would of course contribute to the rent, and I can help in other ways so that you and Joseph are free to write and to paint –"

"I was only concerned with your comfort," Keats interjected; "not ours." His smile had grown. "I'm sure we were both hoping you'd stay."

"Then I will," I said. And it was settled.

I was trying once more to read the play *Othello*, and getting nowhere at all. Some of it was perfectly understandable, but I had no stamina for reading verse, and could never quite reach the third scene.

When I threw the book down on the sofa yet again, Keats took pity on me. "Maybe I should read it aloud to you. Would that help?"

"Perhaps."

Keats' smile became mischievous. "In fact, maybe Joseph and I should give you a potted performance. *The Ten Minute Othello*."

"*Othello: The Good Bits*," Severn supplied with a laugh.

"Yes," I said with great conviction.

"We'll invite Dr Clark," Keats continued. He and Severn were silently conspiring with each other, their eyes glinting with glee. "Give us a day or two, Andrew, and we'll see what we can do."

Our amateur theatricals were staged the next evening. Dr Clark and I settled onto the sofa to face Keats and Severn, who stood before the window, each with a bag of props beside him. They solemnly took their bows, and we applauded.

Then Keats put on a black hat, while Severn donned a purple feathered monstrosity that must have belonged to our landlady. Keats turned to face Severn. "I hate him!" he cried. "Othello promoted that mathematician Cassio over me, Iago, his most loyal and professional solider."

Severn responded, "*Then I would not follow him.*"

"*I follow him but to serve my turn upon him.*" And Keats intoned with dark significance, "*I am not what I am.*"

Severn dropped the purple hat, and slung round his shoulders a red velvet jacket I had not seen before. "*What is the matter there?*"

"*An old black ram is tupping your white ewe.*"

"*Oh, who would be a father?*" Severn wailed.

And so they continued. Keats threw my uniform coat about his shoulders and brandished a walking stick as a baton to represent Othello himself, required to explain his relations with Desdemona. "*Her father oft invited me, and asked me to tell the story of my life. She loved me for the dangers I had passed, and I loved her that she did pity them.*"

Severn signified Desdemona with a red shawl. "*To Othello's honours and his valiant parts did I my soul and fortunes consecrate.*"

Then Severn swapped the shawl for the black hat, and as Iago insinuated to Othello, "*O beware, my lord, of jealousy. It is the green-eyed monster… Look to your wife. Observe her well with Cassio.*"

"*I do not think but Desdemona's honest.*"

Iago reminded him, "*She did deceive her father, marrying you.*" After planting this seed of doubt, he persuaded Desdemona to innocently plead Cassio's merits to her husband, and then fabricated physical proof of their supposed affair by planting Desdemona's handkerchief in Cassio's rooms.

The end became an inexorable descent. Othello asked his wife to pray. "*I would not kill thy soul.*" Despite her pleas and protests of honest innocence, he smothered her.

Yet with her dying breath she said, "*Commend me to my kind lord.*"

The truth was revealed, and Othello in shame and despair killed himself.

Iago's fate was to be led away to torture, yet he declared, "*Demand me nothing. What you know, you know. From this time forth I never will speak word.*"

The two players took their bows to generous applause, and then Severn set about putting away the props.

"*I am not what I am,*" I repeated. There was something about the statement that sent a shiver down my spine. "What does that mean?"

Keats just shook his head slowly, as if unable or unwilling to comment. He settled down, resting his head on the back of the sofa, obviously tired.

But he was happy, and his eyes shone, even when he was racked by one of his coughs.

Dr Clark was watching him closely, and his face hardened when he spied a drop of blood on Keats' handkerchief. "How are you feeling?" he quietly asked while Severn was busy in the smallest of the three rooms, still sorting out the props.

At first Keats just shrugged with a hint of irritation, but then after a moment he turned towards Clark and politely replied, "A little stronger every day. Though the gain isn't much when I consider where I started from and how far I have left to go." He smiled at me before whimsically commenting, "But then we're not all blessed with Mr Sullivan's rude health."

"The climate here in Rome *is* beneficial," the doctor observed. "I have based my practice here for good reason."

"Of course," Keats murmured, though he was looking at Clark with some scepticism – hardly unwarranted when you considered how short a time it was since we arrived.

Clark stood up, and brushed one hand against the other, before continuing, "Well, perhaps your situation wasn't quite as serious as we all feared."

Keats looked askance at this, patently disagreeing. However, he stood as well, and accompanied Clark to the door. "No doubt you're right. Another few weeks here, and I'm sure I'll be fine."

"Thank you for the night's entertainment," Clark said as he shook Keats' hand. "It's been very… Good night!" he cried, before acknowledging me with a nod. "Good night, Mr Sullivan."

I barely managed to return his nod before he was gone. In shock, I watched Keats as he made his way back to lie on the sofa with his feet up on one of the chairs. "You don't mean to tell me," I said quietly for fear of alerting Severn, "he is done with you?"

"It seems so, yes."

"But you… John, you are not well. You know even better than I do that you are not well enough to be without medical assistance."

"My fate rests in the hands of Apollo. I am content to leave it there."

"John –" I said shortly. "You must take this seriously."

He considered me for a long moment. Those bright, intelligent eyes of his were sharp in a face that was pale and damp with exertion. "I have my own advice, and am following that of your Mr Bannon. That will suffice."

"John, if I may speak as your friend –"

"Andrew," he said quickly, as he heard Severn returning, "you are a true friend. Give me seven days, and then we will discuss this again."

"If you are no better…"

"Then I will do as you wish."

And I could see that he meant it, so I nodded my agreement.

"What's all this heaviness?" Severn asked as he came back into the sitting room.

"What is our *sole* topic of conversation?" Keats asked in reply.

"Ah, Iago," Severn wisely concluded. And that was that.

Between One Pot of Tea and Another

The three of us sat contemplatively over our cups of tea the next morning. I watched Keats for a while, trying to decide whether and how much to worry about his health. But perhaps the long journey here from England had indeed tired him, and now that he was settled again he was recovering, for he did seem stronger, though still far from well.

He smiled at me when he noticed me watching him, and then sat forward with his elbows on his knees. "Andrew," he said, startling Severn from his tea-induced reverie, "may I ask what your goal here is? I assume you mean to discover more about what this man's intentions are. But are you planning to do something about it, or will you simply report back to Captain Mitchell?"

I acknowledged these excellent questions with a nod. But before I could answer them, I must consider how much more to tell my new friends.

Severn must have intuited something of my reasons for pausing, for he asked, "You don't have any kind of official authority, do you?"

"No, Joseph, I'm sorry. If you are involved, you must be aware that if things go badly, we will only have ourselves to rely on, and whatever my captain can do in a purely personal capacity."

Severn cast a worried glance at Keats, but didn't raise any objections.

"I spoke of state matters," I eventually continued. "Hart stole state papers from Captain Mitchell's home. They weren't just lying around, they were in a secure place; this was a deliberate act. Then, as far as we can discover, he set out directly for Rome. He didn't return to England for Lady Elena's funeral. As yet Captain Mitchell has received no hint of him disposing of the papers. So it is assumed Hart has them here with him."

"What do you think he intends?"

"We don't know. To sell the secrets. To use them as a bargaining tool. To benefit from them in some other way. Nothing is clear."

"But," said Keats, "Captain Mitchell must have informed the British authorities that the papers are missing…?"

"Yes."

"And that he suspects his brother-in-law? Or was that too painful a story to tell?"

"No, he told them that as well."

"Then why do *they* not take action? Why have they not enabled Captain Mitchell to do whatever he feels he must?"

I shrugged uncomfortably. "That is also unclear."

Keats examined me with his sharp eyes before sitting back to ponder this. Severn was looking distinctly uneasy. Eventually Keats concluded, "We need more information."

We asked our landlady, Signora Angeletti, about this Englishman who called himself Iago. "Ah, there's a one!" she exclaimed. "A beautiful animal, that man!" Then she muttered something in Italian and crossed herself. But she would not explain her reaction, nor comment further.

Of course we did not yet know many people in Rome, and it seemed unwise to draw attention to ourselves by asking strangers about Iago, so we decided to enquire at the British Consulate. We were required, in any case, to present our visas there.

Casually, as the clerk was entering our details into his book, Keats said, "There's an English gentleman living near us on the Corso. I understand he is known as Iago."

"Ah, yes..." And the clerk confided, "An eccentric gentleman, if ever there was one. But so effortlessly charming..."

"Do you know him, then?"

"Certainly. He has come here any number of times. In fact, the Consul is holding a reception in his honour tomorrow evening. Much of the English community hereabouts has been invited."

The three of us looked at each other, all sharing the one thought. I left Keats to voice it: "As part of that community, may we attend as well?"

The clerk looked us over very deliberately, and sniffed. "I think not."

"We are English," I avowed, "and we are gentlemen. That must be good enough for any company."

When he saw that I would not back down without an answer, the clerk merely observed, "There is *good*, and there is *good enough*. Tomorrow it is only the great and the good who are welcome."

Keats put a restraining hand on my forearm before I could disprove my own assertion by an act of violence, and he wished the clerk a good day.

The three of us strolled across the Piazza del Popolo the following afternoon, each mulling over our situation. "I cannot believe we are becalmed already," I murmured.

"Will you write to Captain Mitchell again?"

"There is hardly anything new to report, and nothing of significance." I shrugged, feeling ashamed. This was not at all like a battle, where the desirable course of action was plain for any man of initiative to see.

"Perhaps you can ask him for advice."

"Perhaps…" I knew I did not sound enthusiastic.

"But look there!" Severn suddenly cried. "Andrew – that must be him."

Severn had halted and clutched my sleeve. Like an idiot I stalled as well, and gaped in the direction Severn was indicating. It was Keats who kept his head enough to drag us over to the obelisk, and sit us down in its shade as if we were simply weary of the afternoon's warmth.

It was Adrian Hart all right. I had never met him, but there was no mistaking that flow of thick red curls, bright in the sunlight; his hair was heartbreakingly identical to his sister's, though of course cut somewhat shorter and worn with the curls tumbling free. He was tall and elegant and animated. Coolly dressed in greens and blues and crisp white linen.

"He seems to be the perfect gentleman," Severn murmured appreciatively. And even I could admit that Adrian Hart was captivating. We were staring at him, and so were many others in the piazza.

Hart was standing just at the edge of the Corso, talking with a Catholic priest richly swathed in red silks. To be precise: Hart was talking in a relaxed and confident manner, and the priest was arguing, gesturing in frustration. Carriages waited by the steps of the Palazzo Amara, as if the priest had arrived just as Hart was leaving, and Hart had drawn him aside to exchange words. The discussion threatened to become heated for a moment, until Hart smiled in cool acquiescence, and bent his head closer to make a suggestion which was eventually accepted.

And then they parted. Hart strode effortlessly back to his carriage, stepped into it, and headed away down the Corso. The priest was slower to leave, but leave he did at last.

The three of us looked at each other. I was full of hate, but Severn and Keats were full of wonder. "Now I know," said Keats. "Now I see why he makes such an impression on people."

"Lady Elena always made an impression, too," I said, "though she was modest and had a good heart."

"Yes. But if I didn't know what he'd done…" Keats cast a doubting look at me. "I would have taken him for a man of integrity."

"He is not," I firmly averred.

"Definitely an appearance of integrity, yes," Severn said. He seemed to be shaking with nerves. "Yet there was something strange about him…"

"His eyes," said Keats. "His eerie light eyes, and how they catch the sunlight."

Severn continued, "And who was that with him, do you think? He must have been a bishop at least, in such trappings. What dealings should Iago have with a bishop in Rome?"

"A bishop?" I echoed. That meant the kind of power that was out of my league, surely.

"We'll have to discover who he was," Keats said. "And whether he might have any interest in what Iago has to offer."

"The papers, you mean?" I was no longer becalmed; instead, I was sinking. I muttered a vain prayer: "Lord preserve us."

"Amen," my two companions chorused in response, one ironic and the other sincere.

We slowly made our way home. Severn put water on for a pot of tea; we certainly needed our spirits reviving.

As the water started steaming, though, Severn took a shaky step towards where Keats and I sat on the sofa. "Andrew," he said in a strained voice, "would you show us the locket again?" I must have appeared reluctant, for he continued, "I would not ask if I had not need."

I drew out the pouch, and carefully unwrapped the locket it contained. Opened it to display again my true lady and her false brother.

"Do you not see?" Severn whispered. "Andrew, you said that these likenesses were taken ten years ago, and that Lady Elena had matured since then."

"Yes." I looked up at him, puzzled. But then it struck me. I stared down at the miniature of Adrian Hart.

Keats was the one who voiced it: "He has not aged a single day."

I cleared my throat, determined not to succumb to dramatics. "Many people do not appear to age for years, and then it is as if they catch up again within months."

"But it has been a decade! And if anything, he looks even younger now."

"No," I said. I refused to discuss it further.

But I lay awake that night as Severn quietly slumbered, and in the darkness my heart could no longer deny its unease.

Truths of Varying Reliability

The following evening, we happened to dine in a trattoria just across the street from the British Consulate. The great and the good began arriving in their fine carriages from about nine. "Who is that?" we kept asking our waiter. "And who is *that* gentleman?"

The waiter tired of this quickly enough, and sent one of their regular customers out to answer our curiosity. He soon proved to be an incorrigible gossip. We heard all kinds of things we shouldn't about the ladies and the gentlemen, most of whom seemed no better than they might be.

But at last appeared the priest who'd been talking with Hart in the Corso that afternoon. His red robes were now trimmed with gold, in a manner that must appear ostentatious to any Englishman. "Who's that?" asked Severn. "He must be a bishop or something more."

"O-ho!" our new friend cried with a laugh. "Something more than a bishop indeed… *That*, my dears, is also a cardinal." He clearly enjoyed having an audience, and one that he might be able to surprise as well. "More than that, he is charged with the care of the Vatican Library…" Another sweep of our rapt faces. "And more than *that*, he is the nephew of the Pope."

"Ah," said Severn wisely, "so he is family."

This was met with a smirk. "Guido Rinaldi is close family indeed, as the Pope's *nephew*…"

Keats was the first to catch onto his meaning. His lips twisted in a wry smile. Severn dropped his face in his hands, trying to smother a high-pitched laugh. But my heart sank. A son of the Pope, even though illegitimate, would surely prove a formidable ally for Hart.

Last to arrive was the guest of honour. We all watched silently as Hart disembarked from his carriage, resplendent in understated finery. His embroidered mint green satin coat struck my heart through with memories of a particular dress of Lady Elena's.

"And who was that?" Keats asked once Hart had disappeared within.

But our new acquaintance quickly made his excuses, and saluted us in farewell as he strolled away down the street.

The three of us were silent as we wended our way back to the Piazza di Spagna. Rome by night was an intriguingly dangerous proposition, with boisterous laughter on the streets and furtive flights and fumblings in the alleyways. It surprised me, then, when the slight, pale and eternally dithering Severn announced, "Gentlemen, I do believe I will take a detour."

I looked at him in surprise. He gave us a lofty profile as he gazed up at the stars, as if concerned with nothing but the most noble of pursuits. It was Keats' bittersweet and knowing smile that gave me the hint. "Go and have fun, then, dearheart," he said to his friend. When he caught me staring, Keats added, "Go with him, if you like, Andrew."

In many ways I was sorely tempted, and yet I demurred. "No, I'll see you home."

"I can make it on my own from here."

"Nevertheless…"

They knew not to press further. Severn left us with a formal bow, and headed back the way we had come. Keats and I wandered along alone together, silent again.

We reached our rooms, and settled with books in the sitting room. I began reading, but Keats did not even open his volume; instead he toyed with the spherical white stone he kept in his pocket, and considered his thoughts.

Eventually he said, "Andrew, may I tell you something? May I share a secret with you?"

"Yes, of course." I put my book down.

He seemed reluctant and yet compelled. "I only ask because I believe you will understand."

"You can trust me," I reassured him.

He blessed me with a smile. "I have already established that you are the most trustworthy of men."

I muttered something about only hoping to deserve his trust, and that of my captain, as I had done little enough as yet to earn it, but Keats kindly waved me into silence.

"I carry such a burden," he eventually confessed in a whisper. "There is a girl back in England." He grimaced as if there were aspects of this story that he could not bear. "A young woman, beautiful and brave and vivacious… We are engaged, though it is a secret. Her mother has given us her blessing, even though I am hardly a worthy match on any grounds whatsoever." He ground to a halt.

After long moments, I prompted, "And she cares for you, as you care for her?"

He nodded, and those bright eyes of his flashed at me for a moment. Then he lowered his head so his face was obscured, and he cried, "But I am fortune's fool! I know I will never see her again in this life, and I have no hope of any other." And he struggled not to weep.

I could only watch him, unsure of what comfort to offer or indeed if any were wanted. Eventually I carefully murmured, "But you will recover your health, and return to England –"

"I know I will not."

"You *have* been getting better," I argued. "Even Dr Clark said –"

"Clark is a fool, and I wanted rid of him. I know my own symptoms. I have watched my mother and my youngest brother die of the same disease. My training allows me no room for hope."

"But since you have been following Mr Bannon's advice, I have seen an improvement. Even while we were travelling here, with so few comforts, you were better than in Naples."

"I may never be wholly well, so how am I to support us even if I do return? I have little hope of weaning the public from Lord Byron's verses, and I promised myself to follow poetry, to heal with my words, not with my hands. No, I fear I must break it off and vow never to see her again, though it will destroy me to do so."

"John, if she is as brave as you say, then she will not let you give up all hope."

He shook his head in refusal of my opinion, but the smile he offered me was wry. "Andrew, how can you talk so, when your love is as hopeless as mine?"

That stung me into a sharp retort. "*Your* love is alive and unmarried, and she cares for you. Do not you talk to me of hopelessness!"

A peaceful silence fell, and eventually calmed me. I found I was standing at the open window, gazing out at the night sky. A cloud drifted past the moon, while below me the sunken boat burbled on.

Behind me, Keats murmured, "I am sorry, Andrew. I guessed at your feelings, but I shouldn't compare…" He sighed. "Perhaps you understand this as well: Sometimes it is more painful to hope than it is to despair."

"I understand," I said thickly. I turned back to face him. He was clutching the white stone in his hand. "She gave you that?"

"Yes. A cornelian. It cools me when I feel fevered."

"Then keep it with you, and hold it when you can. Be as brave as she is. Dare to hope."

He looked at me doubtfully, but at least he was listening.

"You will regain your health, and return to England. We all rely on it. So, *you* can afford to hope for it."

"All right," Keats said, though I knew he wasn't entirely convinced. "All right." Then he added with genuine gratitude, "Thank you, my friend."

Severn had already started making sketches for a painting. It was to be a large work titled *The Death of Alcibiades*. I must, of course, ask the obvious question: "Who was Alcibiades, and how did he die?"

"A Greek, who lived four hundred years before Christ. He was raised by Pericles, and taught by Socrates, who thought him beautiful. He became a great general, but defected to Sparta, and then changed allegiances again and again. So, even though he eventually returned home to Athens, and was forgiven, he had made many enemies, and eventually he was assassinated."

The sketches showed three men attacking a fourth with knives, against a Classical building and a Grecian landscape. I frowned over the figures. "Do you want some advice?" I eventually asked.

"Yes," he warily agreed.

"Are the assassins meant to be professionals or amateurs? If they knew their business, they would aim *here* and *here*." I indicated the most efficient targets on the naked chest and shoulders of the fourth man. "It doesn't look like they know what they're doing. Chances are he'd survive this."

"I see," Severn said. He was looking at me strangely.

"Knowledge gained," I murmured, "solely in the service of king and country."

I left Severn starting on a new sketch, and Keats reading and making notes, and I headed for the Vatican Library. Of course they wouldn't let me inside; it was reserved for the use of scholars and religious. But I sat in the colonnade across the small piazza before it, as if resting in the shadows – and was intrigued to see Adrian Hart enter. I waited throughout the afternoon before he came out again, and then I followed him as he strode effortlessly all the way back to the Corso. I, for one, was none the wiser for the trip.

I came back to find Keats sprawled facedown on the front steps of our building, and Severn trying to help him to his feet. "What has happened?" I cried in some alarm.

Severn was a mix of anxiety and frustration. "He has been drinking! John, you know you aren't meant to be drinking."

"Claret," mumbled Keats, grabbing hold of Severn's waistcoat, but otherwise collapsing again in a heap on the next step up. "Finest claret I ever tasted…"

I hefted him over my shoulder, and we got him upstairs, lay him on the sofa, made him drink as much water as he'd let us give him.

"He was there," Keats insisted, waving an inconsiderate arm towards the window.

Severn lifted the jug of water out of the way. "Who was there?"

Keats eventually stumbled out the key points of the story. "*He* was there. Iago. In the trattoria across the way."

I frowned. "When? This afternoon? He can't have been. He was at the Vatican Library."

"He was there at an outdoor table."

That made no sense. "Well, I didn't see him come out all afternoon. Unless there's a back entrance to the library. But he would have had to return in the same way, and then come out the front again. I followed him to the Corso from there, not quarter of an hour ago."

"Bottle of claret and two glasses. I sat at the furthest table from him, but I drank his claret. Finest I ever had."

Severn shook his head over his friend, who had half slipped into a doze. "John always did love a glass of claret. But he knows better than to be drinking like this with his health so poor. Maybe one glass as occasion demands, that's what he told me Mr Bannon said."

"I don't understand." But, then, Keats was a poet and must by definition have an excess of imagination. "Is he much given to fancies?"

"Not like this," Severn averred.

We remained perplexed.

Keats remained fast asleep, so eventually I carried him through into his bedroom. Severn took his shoes off, and we gently wrestled off his coat, while he slumbered obliviously. We made sure he seemed comfortably settled, and left him to it.

"Andrew," Severn murmured as we returned to the sitting room, "would you do me the honour of looking at this?" He handed me his open sketchbook. "I would appreciate the truth from your critical eye."

It was another draft for his *Death of Alcibiades*, and this time it was a marvel. "Absolutely correct," I said. "*That* is deadly intent exactly."

"Thank you."

I could hardly tear my attention from it as my gaze roved back and forth and around. There was the most amazing flow of energy within it. "But how do you do that? It has come to life, when it is only lines on a piece of paper."

"Lines, yes, creating forms and paths and rhythms."

"Excellent work, then!" I felt I had just learned something significant about art. Severn was bashful but pleased, and despite my frustrations and Keats' misadventures we both felt content at the end of the day.

The next morning, though, when Keats finally awoke, everyone was out of sorts. Keats continued to insist on having spent a great deal of the previous afternoon sitting across from Iago, while I was equally as convinced that he couldn't have left the library.

Eventually Keats shrugged off this mystery, and posed a greater one: "I think he knows us."

"What?" I exclaimed. "How can he?"

"I think he already knows who we are and that we are not his friends."

"Impossible," said Severn.

"Nevertheless, I am sure he was sitting there at the trattoria waiting for me."

I retorted, "Now I *know* you imagined the whole thing."

A pugilistic flash from Keats' eyes silenced me.

All told, it was not a good day.

The Way Forward

I lingered morosely over a blank piece of paper, with a pen in my hand and a full inkpot mocking me. What could I report to my captain except my failure? My head hung heavy from my shoulders, and I found myself pressing my left palm flat over Captain Mitchell's locket, pressing his lady to my chest.

The others were silent, perhaps respecting my troubled mood. But eventually Keats said, "What do you intend now, Andrew? What plans do you have?"

"None," I confessed. I had initially felt my captain expected more of me than I might be able to give, but that perhaps I could rise to the challenge. Now I was beginning to think his confidence was entirely misplaced.

After a lengthy pause, Keats offered, "I have had one idea."

"Yes?" I turned to look at him, as did Severn.

"We could not attend the reception. You were not permitted to enter the Vatican Library. We do not move in the same circles as Iago, and perhaps we cannot. But I know someone who may well do so."

Severn whispered, "Shelley."

"Just so." Keats looked at me very directly. "We have talked of him before. Mr Percy Bysshe Shelley. A published poet, and the son of a baronet. He would have access to people and places we do not."

"Would he be prepared to come here?" I asked.

"He might. He suggested we go to him in Pisa. He might in turn come to us in Rome."

"And would you trust him with this?" I leaned forward to make my point. "John, this business touches my captain deeply, and me as well. And the fact that state papers are involved, presumably state secrets. Would you trust him so far?"

Keats pondered this for a moment, and then he said, "Shelley and I have not always agreed, but we share a good and true friend, and when Shelley heard I was ill he did not stint in his generosity. I believe you can trust him, Andrew."

"Good." I nodded. "Then if you would…"

Severn seemed pleased with this outcome. "In the meantime," he added, "I thought I might use that introduction to view the artwork displayed in the Palazzo Amara."

I looked at him with great misgivings, which Keats seemed to echo. "Joseph…"

"What harm can be done? Iago does not know me, and –"

"But I fear he does!" cried Keats.

"– and in any case I would only see the housekeeper. But I thought it might be useful to get a little more of an idea of the place."

"I don't know."

Severn threw up his hands. "I have every right to go there. And I want to! There is a Friar Angelico, a Raphael, and two by Michelangelo! This is not just any private collection, but a significant one."

Keats considered him. "Will it be important for your work?"

"Yes."

He shot a glance at me, and then eventually Keats nodded. "All right. As long as that is the sole purpose of your visit. You mustn't take any risks, or alert Iago any further to our interest in him. I am not only concerned about you, but about Andrew's task here."

This warning threw Severn a little, but he accepted Keats' terms. And so it was agreed.

Keats and I settled at a table outside a trattoria on the Corso that afternoon, and started our watch. A few minutes later, Severn walked past without seeming to notice us. He strode on down the street, his sketchbook under one arm, and then climbed the steps to the door of the Palazzo Amara. We watched as he proffered his letter of introduction, talked with larger gestures than usual. Eventually he was admitted.

A sigh gusted from my companion. "I am sure this is a very bad idea," he muttered. Then he glanced at me with a faint smile. "Perhaps I underestimate Joseph's resources."

"Perhaps," I neutrally agreed.

We slowly worked through a plate of bread, hard cheese and black olives, while I drank a beer and Keats drank a glass of red wine, the latter greatly watered down. An hour passed. Two. Keats forgot about worrying and instead slipped into his own thoughts. I knew he was starting to work on a new poem, and assumed he was mulling over the words or the ideas.

Eventually I noticed a stooped figure shuffling along the far side of the street, close up against the wall as if he couldn't bear to be exposed. Every now and then he sped up, but seemed to have no sense of balance, so after a while of skittering along he'd slow into a shuffle again. I didn't think much of this, except to pity the fellow – until I realised, of course, that it was our own Severn.

"John!" I drew his attention to his friend, and Keats immediately ran off to help him. I took a moment to leave some coins on the table and then followed.

Severn was propped back against the wall of a house when I got there, his thighs tense and quivering. Keats had his hands on Severn's shoulders, examining him anxiously. "Joseph… Joseph… Tell me, dearheart. What is wrong? What has happened?"

"He was there," Severn muttered. His head rolled against the hard wall. It seemed he could not look at us for shame. My heart sank. "*He* was there."

"Are you hurt? *What happened?*"

"Animal. An animal."

"What animal?" Keats was puzzled, trying in vain to meet Severn's gaze, to get some sense out of him.

"It's no use," I murmured. "Let's get him home."

"Papers," cried Severn. "So many papers!"

Keats and I dragged him away from the wall, and each got a shoulder under his arms, our arms round his waist. "Come on, dearheart," Keats said. "Walk with us now."

"Animal," Severn repeated. Then he looked in horror at Keats. "He was an animal!"

Keats just shook his head at this, apparently thinking it nonsense, but it gave me pause. That was how Signora Angeletti had described Hart as well: *A beautiful animal, that man!* I wasn't sure exactly what either of them meant, but it could hardly be good.

We lay Severn down on Keats' bed. He would not let us take off his shoes and coat let alone any other article of clothing, so we draped a blanket over him into which he twisted closely as if it were a cocoon. Eventually Severn sipped a little water that Keats gave him, but otherwise would not be comforted. After a half hour of this, Keats was so worried that he agreed I should fetch Dr Clark.

"And what has upset him so?" Clark drily asked once he'd finished examining Severn. He looked from Keats to me and back again, clearly disapproving. "What have you gentlemen been up to?"

"Nothing," Keats replied with unveiled exasperation. "He went to a palazzo to view the art in their gallery. He had a letter of introduction. Later, we found him in the street like this. We don't know what happened."

"I see." Though of course he did not, and he rightly suspected we knew more than we were telling. "And how long has he been like this?"

"It's almost an hour now since we got him home," I supplied. "We don't know how long before that." I suddenly had the most awful image of Severn crouched trembling in an unseen corner of Hart's palazzo, until finally he brought himself to break away and stumble down the Corso towards his friends.

"Well, I have given him a few drops of laudanum to calm him. Otherwise he seems physically unhurt. Make sure he rests, gentlemen, and I will call again this evening."

Clark was about to bow and walk out, but Keats stopped him with a desperate question. "Can you not tell –? Is there no clue as to what happened?"

"None, I'm afraid." Clark considered him now with a little of his earlier kindness. "Let him rest, Mr Keats. Make sure he feels secure. The attack will pass and his nerves will calm."

"Thank you," Keats replied.

I saw Clark to the door, and returned to the sitting room. Keats was just coming back from the bedroom. "How is he?" I asked.

"Asleep."

"No doubt the best and only thing for him to do."

Keats paced up the length of the room and back again, his hands clenched into fists. Then he turned and gazed at me. "Andrew. What on earth can have happened? What do you know of this man? *What has he done to my friend?*"

"I do not know."

"Did you expect something like this? How could you have let him go there? And all alone!"

"I am sorry, John," I cried, feeling just as frustrated and angry and impotent as Keats must. "I assumed it would all come to nothing!"

He glowered at me, and again paced up the room and back. "What do we do now?" he eventually demanded.

"I do not know that either."

The glower became truly pugnacious. "My inclination is to go there and get the truth of all this from that man. Give him as bad a scare as he has given poor Joseph. But *that*, I suppose, would be showing our hand."

"It would." Though I could not think that we held any cards at all in this game, or if we did then only very weak ones.

Keats seemed to agree. He stopped at last with his back to the window, and sighed. "I have a horrid suspicion that Iago already knows our identity, our location and our purpose. And yet it still seems fruitless to give anything away that we don't have to."

"I cannot think he knows us, but I agree with your conclusion."

So, stymied and silent, we stood or paced around in the sitting room until it turned dark and Dr Clark returned. He forbore commenting on our lack of lit candles.

From the following day Keats and I each began to take turns to follow Hart around, while the other took care of Severn. We didn't learn much from Hart's movements, and saw little improvement in Severn's condition. It was a disheartening time.

Hart socialised and took the air and drank wine at the outdoor tables of numerous trattoria. He was a prodigious walker who often left his carriage at home or sent it on without him, despite which he always seemed to arrive at his destination with his britches and boots unmuddied, his coat unwrinkled and his linen pristine. The only serious thing he seemed to do was visit the Vatican Library, and we still had no real idea of what he did there.

Meanwhile, Severn soon became well enough to get out of bed and sit on the sofa, still snugly wrapped in a blanket. But he barely spoke, and certainly never about his visit to the Palazzo Amara. He read a little, but though Keats and I constantly encouraged him to return to his painting, Severn didn't even scribble let alone sketch.

On the Friday, I reminded Keats of his promise to again confer with Dr Clark about his own condition, if I thought he had not improved during the past week.

"Then, what is your verdict?" he asked warily.

"I must acknowledge that you seem sound enough," I allowed. "Perhaps it does you good to remain here quietly with Joseph."

"Perhaps."

"Would you tell me truly if you felt in need of Dr Clark's care?"

Keats eyed me for a long moment, but eventually he said, "I would, and for now I do not."

"All right," I said, though I had misgivings.

"All right," he said in satisfied tones, as if he had none.

Arrivals – December 1820

On the morning of the first day of December, there was a thundering at the door, and in strode a tall thin man with wild brown hair, perhaps in his late twenties. His shirt was open at the neck, and he wore a long overcoat of a dull blue colour. On any ordinary man, I might have suspected the latter garment of having once been a fine silk dressing gown; on the son of a baronet, it must obviously be taken as acceptable outer wear. For this was Percy Bysshe Shelley, blown in with the new month on a gust of cold wind.

"Gentlemen," he greeted the company. He shook hands with his friends. "Keats, how d'you do? Severn, how frightful you look! I thought *you* came along to take care of poor Keats here." He turned back to Keats and considered him carefully. "Though you are looking better than I feared."

"Thank you," Keats calmly replied. He introduced me, and Shelley shook my hand.

"Now, what's all this excitement? With what do you need my help?" Shelley clasped his hands together in glee. "It sounded quite dramatic! Yet you did not send me any details; it was all very vague."

I was relieved to hear it; the country was full of unrest, and if our letters were intercepted we did not want them completely understood by anyone.

Shelley was continuing, "So I left Mary to sort out the rooms at the hotel, and came around directly to solve the mystery."

At which moment a letter arrived for me. I recognised Captain Mitchell's handwriting, so indicated that Keats should fill Shelley in while I read my letter.

When I was done, I sat there in silence while Keats and Shelley talked on. My heart beat heavy in my chest. For I found I had failed.

Eventually Keats reached the present day in his tale, and somewhat later Shelley ran out of questions, and then they took notice of me waiting there. "Andrew. What's the matter?"

"I have failed. At least on one point. I took no action, and events have overtaken us."

"What is it? What has happened?"

"Lord C—," I replied. "The papers that were stolen involved him in some way, I don't know exactly how. There was some implication… He has tried to kill himself. He survived the attempt, but his condition was still precarious when the news reached Captain Mitchell."

Keats and Shelley exchanged a look. "Well," said Shelley, gently for my sake yet quite blasé, "no one likes that man. Most despise him. No one would miss him were he burning in Hell now."

"That is not the point," I stiffly replied. "I am aware that Lord C— has a difficult character, that he is unpopular, but no one deserves to be driven to such desperate lengths."

"Andrew –" said Keats.

But I continued quite forcefully: "Adrian Hart leaves death in his wake, and no one truly deserves that." And I turned my back on them and walked out of our rooms. I must have walked along every single path on the Pincian Hill before I was prepared to return.

I accompanied Shelley to the Vatican Library the next day, and was suffered to wait in the vestibule while Shelley was welcomed within. It seemed that Keats' idea of involving the son of a baronet was already proven worthwhile.

After an hour or so, Shelley swept past me and out through the doors. I hastily followed him, ran across the piazza and down the street to catch up with his long-legged stride. Shelley was fuming. "What is it?" I asked. "What has happened?"

He turned on me. "Even I am not permitted to enter the Secret Archives."

"The Secret Archives?" I echoed in bewilderment. "There are Secret Archives? How do you know about them?"

"Everyone knows they exist," Shelley retorted, before striding on. "Almost no one is permitted entry."

I was still mentally scrambling, and had no idea why he was so angry. "But you tried to enter…?"

Shelley stopped abruptly and turned on me again. "*He* was there. Your man Iago. I recognised him immediately."

"But –"

"Exactly. They just let him in. And, more than that –" Shelley took a breath, and regained a little self-possession. He continued in a more reasonable voice. "It works thus, Mr Sullivan: If you want to see a document from the Secret Archives, you have to ask for it specifically. You have to already know that it exists and that it's there. You must already know the secret. Then they bring the document to you in a separate reading room."

"All right," I said, indicating that I understood thus far.

"Not so with your Iago." Shelley took another breath and leaned close. "He was *in* the Archives, I saw him through the doorways. *And he was browsing the shelves.*"

I frowned.

"*No one* has that kind of access. None but a cardinal or two and the Pope himself. No one!"

We returned to our rooms, and Shelley told the story again while pacing back and forth. Keats stood propped against the windowsill, while Severn sat bundled up on the sofa, too distracted to pay much attention.

When Shelley was done, Keats asked the obvious question: "What was he looking for?"

"I have no idea," Shelley replied in frustration. "I tried asking the librarian what was there, but of course it was no use."

"Andrew?"

I shook my head. "We are no closer to knowing his intentions. I am beginning to think that we never will." My captain had chosen the wrong man for this task.

"What was in the state papers he stole?" Shelley asked. "Would he be looking for information related to those?"

"I do not know."

"Did you *ask*?"

"No. I thought it better to be discreet."

Shelley shrugged impatiently, and restrained himself from replying. He and Keats and I were silent for a moment.

"Papers," Severn was muttering to himself. "Papers… So many papers." He sounded a bit crazed. Keats looked on him with pity.

But Shelley cast Severn a dismissive glance. Which annoyed me, perhaps all the more because I myself had once been equally dismissive of Severn. I picked up Severn's sketchbook from where it awaited him on the sofa, and leafed through to find the marvellous draft he had made for his painting;

this would prove Severn's worth. But I could not find it. "Joseph, where is that sketch you made? The brilliant one for *The Death of Alcibiades*. I think Mr Shelley would appreciate it."

Severn shivered, and curled up further. "Gone, it's gone."

"Where? Is it in your studio?" I thought perhaps it was in the third of our rooms, which Severn had set aside for his artwork.

"No, *he* took it. He was there, and he took it."

I frowned over this, but there was only one possible meaning. I remembered Severn waiting on the steps of the Palazzo Amara with his sketchbook tucked under his arm. "Hart took it? Iago?"

"Shame," Severn murmured. "The shame of it."

Severn and I had formed the habit of attending a Sunday service read by an Englishman resident in Rome, the Reverend Mr Wolff. While Severn had missed the previous week, he seemed keen to attend again despite his continuing weakness, so we walked slowly to the house where the service was held. Severn sat through it with his eyes closed, though he was obviously awake for his face was lifted towards heaven. But he did not seem to take his usual solace from the service nor find any peace.

When we returned to our rooms, Keats announced that he would call on Mrs Shelley, and asked if I would like to accompany him. "I would," I replied, "but I had better stay with Joseph."

"No," Severn protested, "I will come, too."

"Are you equal to it? We will need to climb this stairway." Keats indicated the steps that led up far beyond the height of the house in which we stayed.

"You haven't set foot outside these rooms until this morning," I reminded him. Not since his disastrous visit to the Palazzo Amara.

"Does a gentleman weigh such things against his duty to a lady?" And he offered us a watery but still genuine smile.

So it was that we three made our way to Shelley's hotel amid the clanging of church bells. Drifts of people mingled on the steps and passed us on the streets, some in finery and others in penitent black. We found the hotel with little trouble on the Via Veneto.

Mrs Shelley received us alone. She was a fine looking woman, with her long light brown hair tightly drawn back from an elegant face. Her manner was polite yet friendly, reserved though not stilted, and she seemed quite mature, even though she must have been a few years younger than Keats and me. She greeted Keats and Severn with a warm handshake, and offered the same to me when introduced. Looking directly up at mine, I found her eyes to be as sharp and clever as Keats'. "How d'you do, Mr Sullivan?" she asked.

"I am well, I thank you, ma'am."

She sat on an armchair, and we three all sank onto a long sofa. Keats led the way in conversing about the usual topics travellers air: news from home, recollections of recent journeys, recommendations of where to visit locally, and cautionary tales of what to avoid. Mundane conversation, anyone might think, and yet these two people were both worth listening to.

A little boy toddled in after about a quarter of an hour, and headed straight for Mrs Shelley's lap. She bent a look of concern on him while her hands ran over his head and shoulders as if needing tactile reassurance of the wholeness of what she saw. It was the most animation I had seen in her, but soon she was peaceful again. "Our son," she announced. "We named him Percy Florence in honour of where he was born."

"A beautiful city and a beautiful child," Severn murmured.

"He turned one just three weeks ago." She drew him up onto her lap. "He seems to have taken no harm from our journey."

"I am relieved to hear it," said Keats. He suddenly seemed stricken with worry. "I hope my request for Shelley's assistance here did not greatly inconvenience you."

She smiled at him, though her hands remained firmly on little Percy Florence. "We move about so much, Mr Keats, that a sudden trip to Rome seems quite natural."

It was then that Shelley himself appeared, in his shirtsleeves and with his hair wilder than ever. "Mary! Mary, I cannot find – How d'you do?" he offered distractedly to the three of us. "Mary, I cannot find my brown leather box. You know the one – the small box containing the letters." He lifted his brow and nodded to indicate the serious significance of this object and its contents. "Surely we brought it with us."

"Surely. It travels with us everywhere." Mrs Shelley seemed quite calm.

"I cannot have left it in Pisa. Yet I cannot find it!"

"Sit down and have a cup of tea with us," Mrs Shelley suggested. "We will look for it this afternoon."

"But where can it be?"

"It is probably hidden under a coat or some such. No doubt you threw something over it without realising. Or it is hidden in the corner of a larger case."

"Ah!" He dashed off, apparently having a fresh idea of where the box might be. But he came back empty handed.

Mrs Shelley softly said, "Come and sit down, my dear Shelley. Your friends are here."

He seemed too distracted to pay heed, but moments later a better distraction presented itself. There was a knock at the door, and a man strode in, tall and commanding, with a thick sweep of curly black hair and bright blue eyes. His figure was better padded out than Shelley's, but he dressed accordingly and it suited him. The principal quality one noticed about him, however, was his beauty, which was legendary – so it did not take Shelley crying out his name for me to identify him. "Byron! What the devil are you doing here?"

"I could ask you the same, my serpentine friend. What is this? You slither off to Rome for an adventure without me?"

Shelley was grinning at him. "Yes, how dare I?"

Byron stepped over to Mrs Shelley, and bowed gallantly over her hand. "How do you do, my dear? I am delighted to see you looking well, and the little snake likewise." He ran a hand over her child's locks.

I was a bit surprised by the fondness of Mrs Shelley's calm smile, but I did not suppose that any woman could remain immune for long if Lord Byron wished to charm. "My lord," Mrs Shelley murmured. Then she turned a little to greet a man standing just by the open door. "Hello, Fletcher. Do come in, if you would like to."

"Thank you, ma'am." He was a stocky fellow, with the no-nonsense air of a certain kind of working Englishman. Somehow he managed to be both self-effacing and proud; he stood true and strong as if he knew his own worth. I had known sailors like him on many ships, and they were often her best men. Neither could his manners be faulted, for he bowed gracefully to Mrs Shelley, and nodded at the rest of us. I concluded that if he was Byron's man-servant then his lordship could not ask for a better companion. Though there was quite an age difference; I knew Byron to be in his early thirties, but Fletcher must be in his late forties, if not already fifty.

By this time, Byron was being introduced to my friends. "Mr Keats," he said with a slight bow. "How good to finally meet you, and to see you in health."

"Thank you, my lord." Keats had stood politely, as had Severn and I, but from his guarded stance I could tell there was something conflicted in Keats' consideration of Byron.

"Your fragment of *Hyperion*," Byron continued quite easily, pulling off his gloves one at a time.

"Yes, my lord…?" It was as if not only Keats but the whole company drew in a breath and waited anxiously for Byron's verdict. *Hyperion* was a recently published poem of Keats'; he had once described it to me.

Byron took a moment, and then lifted his chin. "It is a fine thing, Mr Keats. You have grown into your talents."

"I thank you."

"You talk about the gods exactly as I suppose they would have spoken about themselves; you have them speak in exactly their own voices. I see the problem you face in continuing, but I could wish it were not doomed to remain a fragment."

Keats was now beyond words. He conveyed his gratitude with a low bow. And yet he retained a proper self-sufficient dignity, in much the same way as this Fletcher and the men like him had always done so.

The greetings and introductions were concluded, and then Byron turned back to his friend Shelley. "Now, really. Deserting me. Were you even going to write?"

"Of course!"

"Hah! In the event, I learned of your journey from Miss Claire – who also, I may add, does not appreciate being left behind."

Shelley shrugged ruefully, helplessly, but Byron's wry smirk held no regrets. They settled in for what would no doubt prove a long conversation, and Mrs Shelley rang for more tea. Even Fletcher took a seat when invited, though on a dining chair at a respectful distance from the main group.

With a keen sense of these things, Keats stood and politely made our excuses. We had paid our respects, and would now return home. Severn, indeed, appeared quite wrung out.

"Can we come to you tomorrow?" Shelley asked. "Or perhaps meet at the Caffé Greco?" The latter was a popular place on the Via Condotti, the street running between the Piazza di Spagna and the Via del Corso.

"Yes, of course. Whichever would suit you best."

"And in the meantime," Shelley asked, "can I tell Byron the tale of our Iago?"

Keats looked to me. I felt uneasy at the tale spreading, even though I knew we could trust the people in this room. But I had listened to Keats filling Shelley in, and knew that he had been as tactful as even Captain Mitchell might have wished. And then there was the reality of the situation: Byron appeared intrigued, and was obviously Shelley's dear friend, and therefore would not let Shelley rest until he had told him all; I suspected that Mrs Shelley must already know as much as Shelley did. I dared to ask, "Can you promise this goes no further?"

They assented.

"And will you help us, if you can?"

"Yes, of course."

"Then do so, Mr Shelley," I said, "and we will talk more tomorrow."

Pandora and All the Evils of Mankind

"I will consult with the British Consul. No, with the Ambassador himself!" Byron was a-swirl with loud plans, though luckily the Caffé was so busy that no one paid much attention to our conversation. There were seven of us crowded round a tiny table spread with the fixings for coffee and tea: Keats, Severn and I; Shelley and Mrs Shelley; Lord Byron and Fletcher. To be strictly accurate, Fletcher was sitting squarely on a stool at the counter, but he was facing us, within arm's reach, and he listened closely to all that was said. "I cannot believe," Byron continued, "that the Ambassador will not interest himself in this matter."

"You cannot!" I cried.

"Why ever not?" He was affronted, of course, at a mere sailor telling him what he could and could not do.

"My captain – Captain Sir William Mitchell – expressly advised me not to. That must be good enough reason in itself – but if you want further, then you may have already heard how the Consul in Naples tried to prevent Captain Mitchell pursuing this. We have no official sanction or authority. If we try to involve them, we may not only risk our own freedom but perhaps ruin any chance of working against Adrian Hart."

Byron considered me long and coolly, and at last seemed convinced when I would not back down. "Very well, then. I want to meet with this Iago. I want to hear what he has to say for himself."

I looked at Keats in despair. This was already getting out of hand, when my captain had stressed the need for discretion.

"My lord," Keats began, "I hardly think we are in a position to confront him –"

"Perhaps *we* are not, and you obviously have not been so, but *I* certainly am. Just who does this fellow think he is? Who was his father?"

"My lord –"

Despite remaining up there on his high horse, his lordship muttered, "You had better call me *Byron*, Mr Keats." He cast a glower round the table. "You had all better do so, while we are engaged on this task of Mr Sullivan's."

After a moment, my friend suggested, "Then you should simply call me Keats."

"Sullivan," I offered. Having already put aside my proper title, this was no hardship.

Byron and Shelley each nodded a polite acknowledgement. Mrs Shelley smiled in what I already knew was her characteristic manner: cool yet genuine.

"Then tell me," Byron continued in slightly less heated fashion, "what this man is doing here. What are his plans? His intentions? What use has he made of these stolen papers?"

"We don't yet know," Keats admitted.

"We have been following him around Rome," I explained. "He socialises at the higher levels of society. He is known and honoured at the British Consulate. He often visits the Vatican Library, and seems to have some kind of relationship with the Cardinal Librarian, Guido Rinaldi."

"What do you mean by that?"

I shrugged. "Either they are friends, or they are working together, legitimately or not. We have witnessed them argue in the street."

"Conniving over some plot," Byron suggested.

"We don't know."

"Then, what *do* you know?" Byron cried in frustration.

"Not much, I'm afraid," Keats replied coolly.

"I thought this would be easier," I confessed. "When I came here, I thought it would be obvious what Hart's plans are, and I would be able to work against them, undo whatever he had done. But he doesn't seem to be doing anything! It's as if he were just another English gentleman visiting Rome, with scholarly interests."

Severn had been silent all this time, lost in his own thoughts. But now he shuddered, and wrapped his arms around his own chest as if cold. "He *has* done something," Severn quietly asserted. "He rifled through my sketchbook, and he laughed, and he took my best draft from me."

Keats placed a comforting hand on Severn's shoulder, while the others considered Severn with varying degrees of sympathy or bemusement. Neither Keats nor I had told Shelley or Byron what a state Severn had been in after visiting the Palazzo Amara; neither of us had explained that Severn's ongoing weakness seemed to be a direct result of some kind of fright he'd received. Maybe we should have. But the truth was we had no idea what had actually happened that day. It seemed clearer now that Hart had committed some kind of assault on poor Joseph; but I was unsure whether the principal harm done was physical, emotional or intellectual.

"My lord," Fletcher murmured into the lull. He was consulting a large pocket watch.

"Very well." Byron stood, and drew on his gloves. "Forgive me. I am expecting a delivery at the hotel. You are welcome to join me there, if you will, and take more tea."

Severn said he would return home, but refused an offer for Keats or me to accompany him.

Shelley also said he'd take his leave. "All is still confusion," he added.

"Still haven't found your box of letters?" Byron asked.

"No." Shelley grimaced. "I would have decided by now that we must have left it behind in Pisa, if it were not for the fact that I have the clearest memory of seeing it in our luggage when we arrived."

"Then I wish you all the joy of rediscovering it." Byron nodded at him, and ostentatiously bent over Mrs Shelley's hand.

Keats and I stood, and bowed. "Mrs Shelley," I murmured.

"Mary," she offered.

"Mary," Keats echoed with a grateful smile, and he also lifted her hand to his lips, though in a far more straightforward manner than his lordship.

Once the Shelleys had left, I was dismayed to find that Severn had already slipped away. My friend was suffering more than I had given him credit for.

Keats and I accompanied Byron and Fletcher to their hotel on the Corso. As we strolled along, heading towards the Piazza del Popolo, Byron broke our brief silence by commenting that he had dubbed Shelley's missing box of papers Pandora's Jar.

"Jar?" I queried. Even a sailor knew something of Greek legends. "Did not Pandora open a box? And Shelley described the thing as a leather box."

Byron was indulging himself in a small smile of superiority. "A common mistake. In the sixteenth century, Erasmus mistranslated the Greek word *pithos* as box, though it was actually a large jar, a storage jar. Alas, the term Pandora's Box has been with us ever since."

I was interested in this piece of literary history, but Keats seemed rather less impressed. After a moment, he stiffly observed, "I was aware of the distinction, my lord."

"Oh, of course," Byron immediately responded. "Mr Keats, I do apologise for lecturing."

Keats inclined his head to indicate that he accepted the apology. Nevertheless, he remained stiff. "You said you could see why I didn't finish *Hyperion*. Do you attribute my difficulty to my lack of schooling in Greek?"

Byron stopped and faced him. "No, sir, not at all." The man was all sincerity and charm when he wanted to be. I could see why he was so very popular with both women and men. "It is simply that I think you had already told the story you set out to tell. The poem would be about the fall of Hyperion and the rise of Apollo. About the necessity of this change and growth, about the marvels of it despite the grief. Is that not so?"

"It is so," Keats murmured with a wryly appeased smile.

"Then you found you were done, though you had barely started what you thought would be an epic. I am sorry there is not to be more, but I very much like what there is."

Keats bowed graciously, and we continued on our way.

The hotel was, as might have been expected, more sumptuous than any place I had visited before. We walked through a vast lobby of marble and mirrors, and climbed to the first floor. Byron's rooms seemed vast as well; I roughly calculated that the three rooms I shared with Keats and Severn would probably fit five times over in his sitting room, and it was apparent there were at least two other rooms as part of his suite.

Between our arrival and that of the tea Byron ordered, six small but heavy chests were delivered. Fletcher opened them all to reveal a mass of books. I felt amused, but Keats was obviously intrigued; he was visibly itching to go over and inspect them. As Byron cast his eye over the chests, he seemed unimpressed. "They are completely out of order! Why, here is Diderot keeping company again with Rousseau… There will be a vicious spat, and it will all end in tears. And there's that atheist Marlowe hard up against the Bible itself! Whatever might come of such a union?"

Fletcher was clearing the room's two bookcases of ornaments and what must be the hotel's literature. "What d'you expect, my lord," he asked mildly, "when there was so little time to organise our journey? I did not have the time to pack them myself, and must rely on the hotel maid."

"Say no more," Byron intoned.

"I will help shelve them," Keats offered, springing to his feet. "What is your preference, Byron? Alphabetical by author, or by category first and then author, or do you have some other system entirely?"

"Do as you will!" His lordship gestured nobly, and sank into a chair. "Just explain it to me when you have done."

Fletcher and I helped, too, fetching and arranging under Keats' direction, the three of us familiar enough now to be comfortable together in our shirtsleeves. It seemed there were a few hundred volumes. "How long are you staying here?" I asked, mystified. I had understood this journey to be quite unplanned, and assumed it would therefore be of short duration.

Byron shrugged. "Not long perhaps. But – poor Fletcher will confirm it – these accompany me everywhere. Tools of the trade, I suppose."

In the third chest I uncovered a translation in manuscript of Vico's *The New Science*, and retreated to browse it in a quiet corner. I had heard of this work, first published a century before. While it wasn't quite a fit with my own interests in natural philosophy, it was said to include a history of knowledge and a philosophy of thought, by which any man might be intrigued.

A comment of Byron's eventually broke into my reverie. "What a fine figure you have, Mr Keats."

"I thank you, my lord," was the ironic reply.

"You think I jest, but I do not. You remind me of the boxer Jem Belcher. Did you ever see him? He was bare-knuckle champion for three years, but then lost an eye, and retired to keep a tavern. And he died too young, nine years ago now – but he was the finest fellow. Impeccable manners."

"Then I truly appreciate the comparison."

Byron chuckled at this retort. "It is your figure that particularly reminds me of him. He was finely formed, with a low centre of gravity –"

"I *am* aware of my lack of height, my lord."

"– and wonderfully strong shoulders…" Byron sighed. "Keats, it does not matter that you are not as tall as some, when you are so perfectly formed."

A moment stretched, and I looked up to see Keats bow to Byron. "To receive such a compliment from one who is six foot tall, and reputed to have the profile of an angel, is an honour indeed."

Byron laughed delightedly. "The profile of an angel! Did you hear that, Fletcher? And is it true, d'you think?"

"Don't know, my lord," Fletcher gruffly replied, "for I have never seen an angel."

Byron was watching Keats with undisguised interest now, as Keats returned to his task. I had been somewhat prepared for such inclinations by the gossip that always surrounded Byron, though I hadn't known whether to credit it until now. Fletcher was noticing Byron's interest, too, and after a long dry stare at his master he rolled his eyes, as if to say, *Here we go again.* But when he noticed that I had caught him out, he immediately returned to his usual silent stoicism.

Silence prevailed, as we all industriously minded our own business for a time.

Eventually Byron picked up an old thread in our conversation, as if it had never been dropped. "And so we must hope that Shelley recovers his misplaced Pandora's Jar. I dubbed it thus as it contains all the evils in Shelley."

"Evils?" Keats cried. I, too, looked up in surprise.

"Oh yes," his lordship drawled. "All the cruelty of love betrayed and abandoned."

"He said it was letters."

"About his first wife, his abandoned children. Other women he once counted as friends, as sisters. Keats, you know his history, even if it is only whispered of."

"That may be, my lord. However –"

"Deserting his wife, and eloping with Mary from Godwin's house, and living with her for years before they could marry. Mary was only sixteen – and her father adored her, you know! Her father was as besotted by her as any man might be."

"Byron, please –"

"The first Mrs Shelley died by her own hand, in despair. It is said she was expecting a third child."

"As his dearest friend, my lord, I wonder why you must talk so."

"And you think me a hypocrite, I suppose, but I never pretend to *love* anyone. Not even my wife, blast her. If some have chosen to believe what is not so, that is another matter."

Keats just sighed, as if disagreeing with Byron but unwilling to start an argument.

Byron considered him. "Perhaps you can suggest the answer. Shelley believes so in love, he puts all his faith into it. And yet his love seems to always turn into cruelty. Is that not a tragedy?"

"Yes, it is."

"But in the legend," Byron slowly continued, "hope remained in Pandora's jar, and sometimes it is said that she let it out as the only possible way for mankind to deal with all the evils she'd released. So perhaps there is hope somewhere in amongst those letters, too – hope for Shelley's soul."

Keats turned away, and bent over the next chest of books. "But hope can be an evil, too," he muttered, as if to himself. "For it can hurt like the very devil."

Under the Pyramid of Caius Cestius

Keats and I still trailed Hart as he journeyed back and forth from his palazzo. We learned nothing new, however, and as a result our efforts slackened. In fact, we followed his example for a while by concentrating more on seeing the sights of Rome than on any more serious purpose.

The seven adults of our group, sometimes with and sometimes without little Percy Florence, met and conversed, shared a meal, visited Roman ruins and Renaissance palazzos. At Keats' request, we concentrated on galleries and the churches with particularly fine or notable art, and on Severn's twenty-seventh birthday we toured the Sistine Chapel and the Raphael Rooms at the Vatican. But nothing seemed capable of drawing Severn out of his quiet gloom. Even the dark, dramatic, fleshy canvases by Caravaggio – which I often found breathtaking, occasionally disturbing – even these failed to move him. And yet I was sure he'd been fascinated by the Caravaggio collection at the Villa Borghese, which we had visited in the days before Severn's misadventure at the Palazzo Amara.

On the tenth of December, Severn, Fletcher and I attended Sunday service. When we emerged from the house, we found a carriage awaiting us in the street, with Byron at the window. "If your souls are refreshed now," he cried, "then join us for some more prosaic sustenance." When he saw Severn looking a little doubtful, Byron explained, "We are to dine in the country. I have organised a hamper full of provisions." Now Fletcher was looking doubtful as well. "Maybe not as magnificently as you would have done," Byron told him, "yet good enough, I am sure. *You* can ride atop the coach!"

Fletcher actually had the best of it, sitting up there next to the driver, for it was an unseasonably clear day, though still cool. The six of us adults who were crammed inside, with Percy on his father's knee, could only gaze longingly at the sunshine outside the windows as we rattled through the streets and out into the surrounding meadows.

Soon the carriage stopped by looming ruins of the old Aurelian Walls that used to surround and defend Rome. We all climbed out and looked around while Fletcher helped the driver lift down the hamper. It was a delightful spot. Sheep and goats grazed calmly on the long grass, with trees spaced about as if in a natural park. Beyond some scattered graves, a narrow marble pyramid rose tall and unexpected in the midst of the weathered reddish-brown stone of the city walls. The air was brisk, and delightfully fresh; I drew in grateful gulps.

Byron's dismayed cry broke the peace: "Oh, *Shelley*, my dear Bysshe…"

I turned to see Shelley on his knees, arms around Mary's waist and face pressed against her stomach. Mary was standing tall, yet tears streaked her face. "It's the first time we've returned," she explained.

"William is buried here," Byron said, as if it were only now falling heavily into place. "I am so sorry."

Mary murmured, "Our dear little Willmouse."

Fletcher carefully approached the Shelleys. "I am very sorry, ma'am. Shall we be on our way? We can have the carriage all set again in a moment."

Mary stroked her husband's hair, until he looked up at her. A silent communication passed between them, and she nodded. "Thank you, Fletcher, but now we are here we will pay our respects."

Shelley got to his feet. His face was as damp as Mary's. They started to make their way hand-in-hand towards the graves, and we all slowly followed them. Little Percy was happily weaving his stumbling way amongst us, oblivious to his parents' grief.

Eventually we stood at a plain marble stone set flush in the ground, almost right at the foot of the towering pyramid. "Eighteen months ago," Mary said quietly, "he was taken from us by a fever. He was only four."

"He was the most precious child," Shelley added. "Always happy, always laughing. As if he'd been blessed by the sun god. We all adored him."

No one else said anything, so eventually I offered, "His beauty is now part of this beautiful place. His laughter is part of its peace."

"Yes," said Shelley.

Very tentatively, I added, "His immortal part – but perhaps you do not believe in such a notion – his immortal part is in a place more beautiful still."

"You are right," said Shelley, turning away. "I do not believe in heaven." He sighed, and clasped Mary's hand again. "Yet, if it is true for anyone, then it must be true for our little Willmouse." And he led his wife back to where the driver had been unpacking the hamper. Fletcher followed close after them, his hat still in his hands. The rest of us each wandered along behind.

Shelley lay stretched on his back, with his head resting in his wife's lap, and Mary gently stroked his hair. Neither of them ate much. Eventually Percy grew tired of running around, and fell asleep curled up under his father's arm. The rest of us sat about in a loose circle, gazing around at the country and the ruins. Our talk consisted of little more than, "Pass the bread, would you?" and, "Here, try some of this." The days were rapidly shortening now, and the sun soon began lowering. We would not have long before the afternoon turned cold.

While we yet lingered, I asked, "Who built that pyramid, and why?"

Byron turned to consider it. "Some Roman named Cestius; it's his tomb. It dates back to the decades before Christ. No one knows anything else about him, so he was probably only notable for the size of his wallet and his ego. It's quite astonishing, isn't it?"

"Yes." Astonishing was exactly the right word. From a narrow yet sturdy base it rose to an immense height, smaller yet far steeper than the Egyptian pyramids I had seen pictured. I could hardly quit marvelling at it.

Apparently Byron was now in the mood for conversation, for he looked about, bypassed the Shelleys, and fixed on the next man along. "Keats. What are you working on at the moment? What are you writing?"

Keats' gaze remained lifted to the blue sky for long moments, but eventually he sighed and looked at his interrogator. "I am reading Milton again."

"Good."

"*Comus*, in particular."

"Yes...?"

Another sigh. "I am thinking of telling the story of Sabrina."

"Ah! Sabrina, goddess of the Severn!" Byron chuckled. "The river, that is." When Severn remained unmoved, he intoned, "*Under the glassy, cool, translucent wave...* Why use just one sturdy noun when you can use three adjectives as well?" Meanwhile, Keats waited with some trepidation. And just as Keats was beginning to relax, Byron let out a derisive snort. "Sabrina, the defender of female chastity?"

"Just so," Keats acknowledged stiffly.

"Well, I do hope for *my* sake that your readership contains very few young women. You will spoil all our fun!"

"Then you doom me to poor sales." Catching my puzzlement, Keats explained, "The reading market for poetry is mostly women."

Byron sighed, and allowed, "You are targeting them wisely with such stories."

Keats acknowledged him with a small bow. "For your sake, I will endeavour to be unpersuasive, my lord."

Byron and Mephistopheles

Byron and Fletcher accompanied Keats, Severn and me to a church on the far side of the Piazza del Popolo, which boasted a chapel designed by Raphael and two paintings by Caravaggio. One of the latter portrayed the crucifixion of St Peter in suitably excruciating detail. Severn did not seem comforted, and still kept his own counsel.

As our group strolled back across the piazza, heading for Byron's hotel, both Keats and I were feeling at a loss. That may explain why it took us a while to recognise what should by then have been a familiar figure. The first we knew of it, Byron had murmured admiringly, "Who is that man?"

The rest of us looked up, or belatedly paid better attention, and saw the sun glinting off red hair atop a fine blue coat and long sage green trousers. "That is him," Keats said, low. "That's the man who calls himself Iago."

We had all stopped and were staring, so it was just as well Hart was walking away from us. It seemed he was on his way to his palazzo, cutting across the piazza from the western entrance. Fletcher was frowning purposefully at the man, but Byron – Byron was gazing at him with fascination. "Upon my word," he breathed, "I hardly know whether my compliments are due to his figure or his tailor. Maybe it is both! What a striking sight that man is."

I glowered at Byron as pugnaciously as Keats might. "Adrian Hart has done great harm to people I care about."

But Byron would not be diverted. "Even so…" he murmured as his gaze followed Hart all the way up the steps into his palazzo. "Even so," he declared once Hart had disappeared inside, "what a splendidly beautiful creature he is!"

And I, not being as literate as my poetic companions, simply growled in response. If Byron must admire a man's figure, I could almost wish it belonged to my dear friend Keats rather than Hart.

Keats received a note from Fletcher early the next evening as we were beginning to think about tea. We were all aware that this was odd, so Severn and I waited with interest as Keats scanned the few lines. "Fletcher asks us to go to Byron's hotel."

"Does he say why?"

"No. And it seems that Fletcher himself is asking, not Byron." Odder and odder.

While Severn was as curious as any of us, he said he would stay behind for the sake of a quiet night, so Keats and I headed off towards the Corso without him. We knocked on the door to Byron's room, and Fletcher opened it a moment later. Before we could go in, though, he murmured, "Thank you, sirs. If I can presume further, it's better he don't know I sent for you."

"All right, Fletcher," Keats said.

"But if he knows, he knows. There's no need to lie on my account."

Keats and I each nodded, and I said, "Thank you, Fletcher." We walked into the sitting room, and Fletcher closed the door behind us. I was just about to ask why he'd requested our presence, when Byron strode in from one of the other rooms.

"Ah, Keats. Sullivan. How do you do?" His lordship looked self-conscious, and then a bit defiant. "I'm afraid I'm just going out." And he was indeed all done up in his finery, with a fancily embroidered waistcoat and an extravagantly tied cravat.

"We called on the off chance –" Keats began.

Fletcher had gone over to help Byron into his coat. "Seeing as your friends are here," Fletcher said bluntly, interrupting Keats, "why don't you tell them where you're going?"

Byron shot a glare at his man-servant. Although his continuing self-consciousness undermined him, he growled, "Mind your own business."

"You *are* my business, my lord. And I don't like to see you take such risks."

"For God's sake! What risk is there in a social call?"

A stone had settled heavy and dry in the pit of my stomach. Not bothering to smooth my tone of accusation, I said, "You're going to the Palazzo Amara, aren't you?"

"Yes." His lordship met my gaze for the first time since he'd walked in, though it was still with a trace of defiance. "What of it? I am entitled to call on any man. *I* need no introduction."

"You are visiting him *alone?*" I could hardly believe what I was hearing. "It's not that he's hosting a supper, or some kind of gathering…?"

"Exactly." Byron gestured impatiently at Fletcher. "My gloves, man."

"No good will come of this. Indeed, you will do us harm," I said, getting angrier and angrier.

Byron huffed. "What possible harm can I do? I may well discover something of use to you."

"That's what Severn thought when he went there. And you have seen how reduced he is now!"

Fletcher asked quickly, "What happened to him, sir?"

I glanced at Keats, but neither of us could answer exactly. "We don't know, but he was so badly shaken he took to his bed for days, and has never been the same since."

Byron rolled his eyes. "With all due respect to the redoubtable Mr Severn, I think I am made of somewhat sterner stuff."

"My lord, if there is some danger –"

"The man is a villain!" I cried. "Not only did he steal those papers from my captain's house, but he – he –" *Forgive me, my lady*, I prayed. "He put such shame and despair in my Lady Elena's heart – in his only sister's heart – that she took her own life. Can you not understand? This man leaves naught but death and destruction behind him. And you want to *befriend* him?"

For long moments Byron stared at me, obviously taken aback at being spoken to thus. But though he seemed to have heard and understood my warning, he was also affronted, and his pride was piqued. There would be no stopping him. Eventually Byron said, "My –" He had to pause to clear his throat, though he still spoke roughly. "My gloves, Fletcher. And my hat."

"My lord," Fletcher asked even as he handed over Byron's gear, "at least let me come, too. You may be glad of my company before the night is through."

"No. No, that won't be necessary." Byron seemed a little shocked. Perhaps I had at least succeeded at putting him on guard. He bowed to us stiffly, and then walked out of his rooms without another word.

We three remaining watched him go, and then looked at each other, wondering what to do now. "Would you stay?" Fletcher asked, his voice as rough and shaken as Byron's had been. "I mean, sirs, I would be glad of your company this evening, and perhaps his lordship will be, too, in the end."

"Of course," said Keats.

"I will pour you a drink, if you like. Or I will order tea. I, uh –"

I found that I had collapsed onto the sofa. Perhaps I was not so complacent about confronting a lord as I'd thought. "A drink, Fletcher," I said. "Thank you. I've entirely lost my appetite."

We waited, anxiously. The three of us didn't talk much, but I'm sure we were all trying to imagine what was happening at the Palazzo Amara. Fletcher kept watch at the windows, from which we could just make out the palazzo's façade further down on the eastern side of the street, but of course there was nothing to be seen.

After almost two hours had passed, there was a knock at the door. We all started up, wondering who on earth it could be. I was afraid that if there was news, it could only be bad. Fletcher went to answer.

But it was only Severn and Shelley. Fletcher wordlessly let them in to join us. I sank back onto the sofa, and Fletcher returned to the window.

"Joseph," Keats said with some concern, "what is wrong?"

I belatedly paid attention to the new arrivals, and saw that they both appeared rather unnerved. "Has something happened?" I asked.

"No," said Severn. "No. But Shelley came around this evening, and we got to talking."

Shelley announced, "I think Iago has taken the box of letters I am missing."

"What?" I cried in disbelief.

"After talking with Severn about what happened with his sketch, I am sure of it."

"How could he possibly…?" I laughed. I'm sorry to say I laughed derisively. "Your letters went missing only a day or two after you arrived in Rome."

"Yes."

"So how could Hart have known? About you, or the letters, or the box, or what it contained. Let alone – He could have had no idea that you would join us and become a threat to him."

Severn and Shelley exchanged glances, and Severn argued, "Shelley came to visit us as soon as he arrived, and if Iago was watching our lodgings, as I think he was —"

"Oh, be reasonable!"

"John said that Iago was waiting for him at that trattoria across the piazza."

I looked at Keats, who shrugged a little and shoved his hands in his pockets, as if unwilling to weigh in on either side of the argument. I turned back to Severn and Shelley, who were standing together by the fireplace. "Look," I said in somewhat calmer tones, "it makes no sense, anyway. Where is the logic in taking the best part of you, Joseph, and the worst part of Shelley? What could possibly be his purpose?"

"But we don't *know* his purpose," Shelley replied. "Not yet. It's a mystery! So how can you talk of the logic behind it?"

Once more I was reduced to no better response than a growl. This was ridiculous!

"Where's Byron?" Shelley asked. Fletcher and Keats explained. And then Fletcher poured more drinks, and Severn and Shelley settled in, and we all simply waited.

When Severn returned from visiting the Palazzo Amara, he had been stooped with dread, and capable of little more than shuffling down the street towards us. When Byron returned to his rooms, over three hours after he'd left, his stance and his gait could hardly provide a greater contrast to what Severn's had been. Byron walked tall and easy, treading lightly as if he were six inches up in the air. He was happy, he was overjoyed, brimming with delight. He came in and beamed around at our flabbergasted faces, as if he had not the faintest conception of the worry and anger and frustration he had caused. "Here you all are," Byron commented mildly, as if content that it should be so.

"Then all is well with you, my lord?" Fletcher asked.

"Of course. Of course." Byron dropped his hat and gloves onto the nearest flat surface, and shrugged off his coat without Fletcher's assistance. "I have had a wonderful evening with a fascinating man."

I stood up with my hands in fists, though I could not find the words. It was Keats who protested, "My lord, after all this man has done –"

"I would have thought you could sympathise. And you, Shelley. He is in exile, deprived of all he has known and loved."

"Oh, he is deserving of great sympathy indeed," I ground out with the heaviest sarcasm, "when any such deprivation is of his own malicious doing."

Byron considered me for a moment, and then turned to Shelley. "Do you remember your Marlowe?" he asked. *Thinkst thou that I who saw the face of God, and tasted the eternal joys of heaven, am not tormented with ten thousand hells in being deprived of everlasting bliss!*"

But even Shelley was not persuaded. "And so you are comparing England with heaven? With everlasting bliss? Whatever happened to your complaints of that *snug little island*, that *right little, tight little island?*"

"It is true, the English do not approve of such a one as me, and never will." Byron sighed, and dropped to the sofa in the place where I had been sitting. I walked away, towards the door. "*Sweet Mephistopheles,*" Byron murmured, "*ravish me with a kiss.*"

"And now you are deliberately misquoting," Shelley observed disapprovingly.

Keats scoffed. "He calls himself Iago, a villain, and you call him Mephistopheles, a devil. *I* say we may as well call him Dionysius, for he plied me with the finest claret."

"But you were not seduced?" Byron asked lightly, though he sounded as if he wanted an honest answer.

"I was not."

Byron sighed again, and it seemed his spirits were finally waning. He rolled the back of his head to and fro against the sofa, and then he looked across at me. "Don't leave us, Mr Sullivan."

"Why ever not?" I asked bitterly.

"I know, I know. *I have been feasting with* thy *enemy…*"

I think I could have happily murdered him in that moment. "Speak plainly, or I *will* leave. I cannot believe I trusted you with the truth of any part of this task that is so near to my heart."

"Well, is this of use to you? There is a room there, a library across the hall from the gallery. It is enormous, the largest private library I ever saw.

And it is full to overflowing with chests and boxes full of papers, mounds of papers."

"Papers?" I asked – even as Severn cried, "Yes!" in recognition.

"They are piled and scattered in no order. Just heaped together with a few random pathways in between. All manner of different papers. Letters, legal documents, manuscripts, notes, drawings, bills – anything you can think of."

"Byron," said Shelley with barely subdued anxiety, "did you happen to see my box of letters there?"

A pause as Byron considered his friend. "No, my dear Shiloh, I did not see your letters." He was almost gentle now. "Do you think he has taken them?"

"Yes."

Byron nodded. "Then we will recover them for you. We will get them back."

Even I fell quiet after that solemn promise. Soon the party broke apart and went its separate ways.

Winter Sets In

The unseasonably fine weather ended in a torrent of rain, and we faced the prospect of keeping to our rooms for the day. "It was recommended that I come here," observed Keats, "for the warm, dry air." This was said with light ironic humour, but he added bitterly, "I should never have left England."

Severn looked at him sorrowfully. But then he picked up his sketchbook for the first time in far too long, and said, "It is the perfect day to work, John. Were you serious about Sabrina?"

"I was."

"Then I will sketch, and you will versify, and poor Andrew will have to content himself with being ignored."

I bowed. "I owe Captain Mitchell a letter. Perhaps your industry will inspire me."

So it was that we spent a quiet day despite my disquiet about what Byron had got up to the night before. But it seemed that Keats was the only one who had anything useful to show for his pains, for Severn idled over several pages, starting again and again and then throwing aside the results, while I pondered whether to confess all to my captain or to remain silent and let things run their course.

Due to the weather and its possible effects on Keats' health, Fletcher had considerately arranged for everyone to meet at our rooms on the fifteenth. It was a snug fit, of course, but no one seemed to mind very much.

Byron kept to himself in one corner, looking lofty one moment, then a bit guilty the next, and finally defiant, as if he knew he had not helped our cause yet would do the same again if he had it to do over.

Once we had all gathered, and settled, and sufficient cups of tea were made, Fletcher stepped forward with his hat in his hands. "If I may make a suggestion, madam, sirs…"

"Of course," I said, echoed by Keats and the Shelleys.

"Then, if our goal is to recover the papers Mr Sullivan has an interest in, and Mr Shelley's letters, and Mr Severn's drawing – I will go and get them myself. I don't suppose that's an action you gentlemen could or should approve of – but by my way of thinking, if this scoundrel has stolen things that belong to us, then we won't be going far wrong in stealing them back."

"Hear, hear!" I cried with a sudden return of enthusiasm.

Despite his master regarding him with withering impatience, Fletcher stoutly continued, "I'm offering to do this whether you approve or not, if you take my meaning. It seems to me that the sooner this is dealt with and the less we have to do with this man, the better all round."

"Fletcher," Byron began in heavy tones, "this is not going to happen."

"My lord, if I –"

"I don't doubt your felonious skills," Byron said drily, "but you would not succeed. The library in that place is massive, and it is *filled* with papers. Were you not listening the other night? There are piles of them. Hundreds of thousands of documents. Even if you could recognise what you wanted when you saw it, you would simply not have time to find it in the first place."

"I'm willing to try," Fletcher replied. "You can tell me where this room is. You know the arrangement of the place, and I will break in one night soon. If it's still pouring like this, the clouds will hide the moonlight, and the rain will drown out any noise I might make."

"And I'll go with him," I added before Byron could raise further objections. "I'd recognise Severn's sketch at a glance, and I've heard enough about the state papers and about Shelley's box of letters to recognise them, too."

"This has seemed such a *noble* quest until now." Byron's tone was venomous. But Fletcher still stood there stoically enduring his master's disapproval. Eventually Byron sighed, and tossed a conciliatory gesture in Fletcher's direction. "Your offer is appreciated, Fletcher." Byron still sounded angry, but also as if he were trying to overcome his anger. "But it will not be necessary. I have a suggestion, too."

"What, then?" Shelley prompted.

"We should make the acquaintance of this cardinal," Byron replied. "This Cardinal Rinaldi."

"Why?" I asked.

"You have assumed that he is in league with Iago. Well, why don't we find out? Because there is a chance that he might not be an accomplice. Indeed, perhaps he is as much a victim as anyone else in this affair."

Byron looked archly triumphant at this revelation, but I did not resent it as much as I might, for he was correct: I had made an assumption that was not sound. "Then –" I began.

"Then I will meet with him," Byron offered.

Yet I could not entirely trust Byron. "Why not Shelley?" I countered. "He could easily create some pretext – he has already visited the Vatican Library on our behalf." I turned to them. "Shelley, Mary, perhaps you could –"

Byron concluded, "The three of us, then."

"But you must tread carefully," Keats asserted, "for we have had cause enough to suspect him. We don't know that Iago hasn't sold those state papers, or bartered the secrets they contain. It's not unreasonable to think that the man in charge of the Vatican's archives would know the value of a secret."

Mary observed, "It does seem strange to me that the Foreign Office has not already secured these papers themselves. Can they be so much less efficient than the Home Office? Shelley and I know all too well that the latter are persistent enough in pursuing their interests."

I suppose I already knew that many of my current companions harboured radical tendencies, but this confirmed it. Naively, perhaps, I felt they nevertheless had England's interests at heart.

"It occurred to me," Keats began carefully, "that there might be a reason behind the lack of interest from the Foreign Office."

"Why do you say that?" I asked. Such a notion hadn't even crossed my mind.

Keats looked at me for a long moment, as if advising me to brace myself. "Perhaps they planned some kind of scheme. Perhaps the authorities intended that the papers be taken. Perhaps the papers are now exactly where they're meant to be."

I was standing. Glaring. My fists clenched. "No!"

"There is no doubt of his complicity and guilt, but perhaps even Hart himself has been manipulated."

"No!" A fraught silence surrounded me while my companions awaited my thoughts. But I was horrified. Could Keats not see the evils he was implying? The situation was infernal enough as it was…

"Andrew –" Keats murmured.

"*No*, I tell you! This has cost my lady her *life*." And I said aloud what I had already sworn in my heart: "Whomsoever is responsible for Lady Elena's death, I will see justice done."

"Even if it is the Admiralty? The Cabinet? The Foreign Office?"

"Even so."

Keats regarded me for a long moment. He could not have found my resolution wanting. Eventually he stood, walked to me, and placed his hands on my shoulders. "I am sorry for the pain of it, my friend."

"As am I."

Fletcher organised more tea as we re-gathered themselves.

The tea was half-drunk by the time Severn tentatively broke the silence. "Andrew," he said, "might I also venture a thought?"

After what had passed I almost dreaded what would come, but I nodded civilly to him. "Of course, Joseph."

"You were sceptical about why Iago should take the best part of me and the worst part of Shelley. You said it made no sense."

"I did, yes."

Severn glanced at Shelley as if for courage; Shelley was naturally enough hanging on his every word. "I have pondered this a great deal. I cannot explain why it should be so, but I feel… I feel as if Iago has taken a part of me. I believe that part of me is now missing."

"Yes!" cried Shelley, shifting to the edge of his seat.

"A *significant* part," Severn added. "I have been… I have not quite been my true self since then."

"So it does not matter whether this thing he took is good or bad in itself," Byron suggested, "only that it means something to you."

"Yes."

"And you feel reduced as a result."

"*Yes*," Shelley averred.

Shelley obviously felt in eager accord with Severn's notion, but I must remind him: "We don't even know for certain that Hart took the box of letters."

"I appreciate that," Mary said in her clear voice, "but I don't know where else they could be. We have searched everywhere. My dear Shelley isn't the most organised of men, but I know we brought the box with us to Rome, and we would have found it by now if it had simply been mislaid."

"Pandora's Jar," Byron muttered to himself. "If this isn't a lesson to us all… I would have preferred to burn the thing myself."

I sat back to ponder Severn's thoughts, and what they might mean. If anything, I felt more confused than ever as to Hart's motives.

Eventually Severn quietly said, "There is something more."

We all looked at him. When he remained silent, Keats said, "Courage, Joseph. You are among friends."

"It is a confession."

"We are your friends, no matter what."

Severn sighed. "Then I must warn you… I feel – I am sure that he took my sketch in return for something. As payment for something."

"For what?" Keats gently prompted.

"At the time I thought it was in return for letting me leave that day. For letting me come back to you."

"Then I am glad of it."

"But since then…" Severn shuddered, and then looked bravely around at each of us. "Since then I have feared… that he is holding it hostage. That he will give it back. In return for… some future action."

Keats was frowning. "What do you think he'd ask of you?"

"I don't know."

Byron scoffed. "What would he want of *you*, Severn?"

"I don't know, my lord." Severn looked up at Byron steadily despite his raw honesty. "What would he want of you?"

And Byron blushed to the very depths of his being.

A Comedy of Errors

Fletcher and I planned to break into the Palazzo Amara the very next night, as it was a Saturday and I knew that Hart rarely spent the evening at home on Saturdays. We conferred together over a birra at a trattoria on the Corso.

"My lord was not very helpful about the man's servants," Fletcher heavily informed me.

"Does he suspect us?"

"I'd say so," Fletcher replied. "But he won't stop me. He's said his bit, and now he'll just sit back and watch for his own amusement."

I'd already sworn to myself that everything would go according to plan, but I would also dearly love to cheat Byron of a laugh at our expense. "Why wasn't he helpful, then?"

Fletcher shrugged. "I can't make it out. He says he can't remember seeing any servants."

"What? Beneath his notice, were they?"

"I put that notion to him, and he just said he honestly couldn't remember. I asked who let him into the place, then, who served them drinks – and he thought about it, and he came up with nothing."

"So we don't really know what we're up against."

Fletcher looked at me. "Begging your pardon, sir, but I was just thinking of avoiding them and getting away again. I wasn't thinking of a fight."

"Of course not, Fletcher."

"My lord tells me you're a naval officer."

"That's right. But even if we're discovered, I wasn't planning on engaging them in battle. I don't want to…" I sighed, and thought about it, but Fletcher of all people would understand. "I am here on my captain's behalf, but it is a private matter. And I do not want to embarrass him."

"Yes, sir," Fletcher said. He left a pause, and then announced, "His lordship was more helpful about the arrangement of the rooms."

"Good."

We met in a dark corner of the Piazza del Popolo just after ten that night, and greeted each other with a silent nod. Fletcher looked grim, resolute, and

I felt much the same. We strolled towards an alley that led away from the piazza, trying to appear casual rather than purposeful, but then once we'd turned into it and were more likely to be free of witnesses we strode along.

Fletcher had left a borrowed ladder tucked away in a cranny between two buildings. We used it to clamber over a wall and into the courtyard of the place next to the Palazzo Amara. Keeping to the shadows, we crossed to the far side, and then used a couple of barrels to help us up onto the top of the next wall.

We lay there for a moment, staying low so we were less likely to be seen against the sky. The palazzo's gardens spread below us, quiet and empty. There were no lights showing from the house itself, except perhaps for a flicker of a lamp from a far window. Fletcher pointed towards our goal: there were three doors along one wall, each made of panes of glass and scrolled ironwork, each opening from the library. I nodded, and we shared a tight smile. That part of the house was completely dark. We could proceed.

I shuffled along the wall for a few feet until I was opposite a mature tree, then used its bare branches to let myself down to the ground. Fletcher appeared beside me a moment later. We headed for the library, using the soft garden beds rather than the gravel paths.

It took Fletcher barely a minute to pick the lock of the door furthest from the rest of the palazzo. I grinned at him and shook my head, impressed by his skills, and intrigued to know where and when he'd had cause to learn them. We each heeled off our boots and left them tucked against the wall beyond the doorstep.

Then we were inside.

I took a few silent steps in my stockinged feet, and almost immediately found myself bumping into a waist-high pile of papers. As my eyes began adjusting to the darkness, I almost let out a whistle. Byron had not exaggerated. There were papers everywhere. Fletcher stumbled into another pile, and sent the top ones cascading to the floor. He looked distraught at such a blunder, but it had hardly made a sound, and no one would notice a slight rearrangement in such a collection.

We had brought handheld lanterns, which we now lit, keeping three sides of the four closed so that the light remained localised. And we began to search, for now concentrating on the papers we could examine with minimal disruption. We kept at it, each going from pile to pile and working our way down the long room, but I soon realised it was an impossible task. Byron had been right again, damn him.

Eventually I drew near the main doors which must lead into the palazzo itself. They were closed, and no light showed under them. I stopped searching, and sighed, stretched my stooped back. The walls were, of course, lined with shelves of books. I glanced along the nearer volumes, imagining the joy of my friend Keats if he were free to browse here.

Something caught my eye.

I stepped closer and lifted the lantern. A sheet of paper hung from the shelves, its corner caught under the edge of a book. It was Severn's sketch, hanging there in plain view. Of all the hundred-thousand papers in that room, it was Severn's sketch. And it was suspended from a book with gold lettering on the spine that read *Principj di Scienza Nuova*. Vico's *The New Science*, that I had lately been reading in manuscript.

Impossible.

Unease crawled up my spine. I beckoned Fletcher over. "He was expecting us," I whispered.

Fletcher nodded glumly, and gestured to the floor. There was Shelley's box. Pandora's Jar. And it had been opened, and was now empty, discarded. All the evils had been released.

I reached to take Severn's sketch, determined to at least return it to him if we achieved nothing else that night. Fletcher shook his head in alarm, and said hoarsely, "If you take that, he'll know we were here."

"He already knows," I replied. And I tucked the sketch away between my shirt and waistcoat.

And then... and then... something strange happened. Even though the doors to the rest of the palazzo remained closed, and the library remained dark, I saw Adrian Hart standing there in the doorway, silhouetted by a blaze of golden light from the hallway. It could not have happened, and yet the fancy felt so real at the time. Inexplicable.

I turned and started back towards the garden door at a sprint – and of course promptly tumbled into a pile of papers. They avalanched to the floor, carrying me along with them. Fletcher, who seemed just as panicked, grabbed me in both hands and dragged me to my feet. We stumbled towards the far end of the room. I had dropped my lantern; it guttered and went out, so all was dark except for the crazy swing of light from Fletcher's lantern. All was dark, and yet I still believed at some level that Hart was standing there watching us. I could see him so clearly in my mind's eye, with his fine figure and his gentleman's attire surrounded by light. It could not have been so.

We made it to the door, and tripped out into the garden. Grabbed our boots. I managed to pull one on, and then hopped off down the path while trying to tug on the other one. Fletcher was behind me somewhere. I reached the tree I'd climbed down, gave up on the boot and threw it over the wall, then started climbing. I fell out of the tree twice, and had to start again. I felt quite mad. I even knew it at the time: a part of me said to myself, *You are maddened. Stop it. Take a breath and start to think!*

There were dogs in the neighbour's courtyard, barking and yapping. Fletcher and I ran across, trying to ignore the lights coming on in the surrounding windows. He boosted me up the wall, and I lay down on it to give him a hand up. Then somehow we managed to fall off the other side, though our ladder waited there offering a bruise-free descent.

The alley was floored with compacted earth rather than stone, but it was hard enough. We lay there moaning for a moment, gathering ourselves. Of course I had left my boot in the courtyard, but we couldn't go back for it now. Eventually we hobbled off, feeling rather sorry for ourselves and supporting each other as best we could. I can only think that the people still loitering in the piazza assumed we were drunk.

We parted on the Corso outside Byron's hotel. And I stumbled home. Crept inside to find that Keats was already fast asleep on the sofa. I lay myself out on my bedroll, then belatedly remembered to slip Severn's sketch out, and place it on the low table by the sofa. I sighed.

My night's adventure, such as it was, had ended. I would have to await daylight to decide whether it had been of any use whatsoever.

When I finally woke the next morning, I found Keats and Severn sitting side by side on the sofa with the sketch on Severn's lap. They were watching me quizzically. I remained where I was, and returned their gaze without commenting.

Finally Keats said, "So you went there. Did you break in? With Fletcher. Or did you make a social call?"

"We broke in."

"Andrew," Severn murmured, "my dear friend…"

"How did you find the sketch?" asked Keats. "Wasn't it as bad as Byron described, with hundreds of thousands of documents piled every which way?"

"He was expecting us. He left that for me to find."

Keats frowned, and glanced at Severn before looking back at me. "What about Captain Mitchell's papers? Shelley's letters?"

I shrugged, and shook my head. *No.*

Severn had been gaping. "Andrew, I can hardly begin to tell you what a difference this makes to me –"

"It's all right," I said. "I'm only glad we achieved something."

"*Thank you,*" he whispered.

And Severn got up, and went to boil the kettle for tea, organise breakfast. A tuneless industrious humming could be heard around our lodgings as Severn began setting things to rights. Later in the day he insisted on a rearrangement so that Keats had the bed again, and Severn would sleep on the sofa. It was almost as if we had the old Severn back with us.

I remained at home all day; I didn't even attend the church service, though Severn went, and said he met Fletcher there. However, if Hart knew of our trespass then perhaps he would arrive to confront me. Surely no gentleman would let such an act go unchallenged. But the hours passed peacefully. On his return, Severn almost seemed happy. I decided the adventure hadn't quite been a total disaster.

Late in the afternoon I caught Keats smiling in some private amusement. When I raised an eyebrow to ask him what it was, he murmured, "*How* many times did you fall from that tree?"

"Only twice!"

"*Only twice,*" he chuckled, sitting back as if watching it all unfold upon a stage. Apparently it was a comedy rather than a farce. So, not a *complete* disaster, then.

Loves of Varying Types

The Shelleys and Byron had visited Cardinal Guido Rinaldi on the Sunday. On the Monday, we all met at the Shelleys' hotel for dinner to discuss what they'd discovered. Well, it was a late dinner for most of us, and an early breakfast for Byron. He demanded dry toast and a pot of tea while the rest of us, with varying enthusiasm, ordered a range of antipasto and pasta or meat dishes.

"His lordship," observed Mary with a smile, "is rarely up before eleven."

"Twelve today," Byron declared. "I was versifying until dawn."

"Excellent! What are you working on?" asked Shelley.

But Byron just winked at him. "Some other time, my friend."

"What of the cardinal?" I asked as soon as I felt I could. "Did you learn anything from him?"

"A great deal," Byron replied, looking particularly pleased with himself.

Cutting to the chase, I asked, "What's Hart trying to find in the Vatican archives?"

"We don't know," Mary replied. "Of course we could not expect the cardinal to be explicit with a group of strangers."

I turned back to Byron in a sudden fit of frustration. "What did you mean, then, that you learned a great deal?"

"We learned something from his reactions," Byron said with maddening calm. "When we mentioned Iago, the cardinal became confused, embarrassed. Very self-conscious. When Shelley said he'd seen Iago in the Secret Archives, the cardinal almost collapsed in fear. There was no attempt made to defend or justify his relationship with this man."

"And so…?"

"The cardinal is a victim as well," Mary concluded. "Iago must hold something over him. Some kind of document, judging by what else Iago has taken."

"You're leaping to conclusions," I argued. "This isn't based on any specific information you've gathered."

"If you'd been there," Mary insisted, "I'm sure you'd have drawn the same conclusion. Iago is blackmailing the cardinal into allowing him access to the Secret Archives."

Severn quietly protested, "How does one blackmail a senior member of the church? Surely a well-respected member of the community, occupying a position of great trust."

Byron looked at him pityingly. "You haven't been in Rome long, have you?"

"The church is corrupt," Shelley asserted. "Why wouldn't it be? Hundreds of years of power and riches beyond that even of kings. No one who possesses all that can remain pure."

"There was some stain on his paternity, was there not?" Byron smoothly supplied before Severn could attempt to mount any kind of argument.

"But the identity of the cardinal's father seems to be an open secret," I said. "If everyone already knows, then where's the leverage?"

Byron shrugged. "There is probably some lingering resentment to be worked upon, even if the man's natural father has assisted him in his career. In any case, there is always the honour and reputation of his mother at stake."

"This is all speculation. Did you ask about the state papers that Hart stole from my captain?"

"We asked," said Mary. "It seemed clear he knew nothing about them."

I looked at her for a long moment. Mary Shelley was cool and sharp and perceptive. It would not have surprised me to be told that she was the most intelligent one of the lot of us. And yet, in this matter, I was reluctant to rely on anyone else's judgement. "I should have been there myself," I said.

"Then we will return in a few days," she replied, "and you will come with us."

"Thank you. Yes."

"It is possible," Mary continued, "that the state papers are still an active concern of Iago's. Even if he hasn't sold or bartered them, or used them in any other way, he may be looking for related information in the archives."

"Yes," I responded, sitting up and gazing at her.

"Perhaps there is a link there. But it depends very much on what was in the papers. May I ask, Andrew – is your concern based mainly on your captain's honour or on your fears for the security of our country?"

"The former," I confessed. "Both, of course, but the former most of all. For me personally."

I regretted once again that I had not pushed Captain Mitchell for more information about the contents of the papers when I could. Restraint and discretion had seemed wise at the time, and an appropriately gentlemanly contrast to Hart's actions. My reticence merely seemed foolish now.

And there was after all reason to consider the papers important in themselves. "A man has already attempted suicide," I reminded my companions, "and we assume it was due to the papers being stolen."

There were dissatisfied shiftings around the table. "Lord C—" Byron muttered. "If only he hadn't bungled that the way he's ruined everything else."

The Shelleys wanted to spend time with their son, and Severn and Fletcher each had business of their own to conduct, so Keats and I accompanied Byron back to his hotel.

On the way, his lordship's eye was taken by a couple of rather pretty servant girls who were gossiping on a street corner. They returned his regard, happy to be admired by a man with the profile of an angel – and apparently no better than they had to be, for they also seemed willing enough for that admiration to be pursued. But Byron turned from them with a sigh. "Did you know, Keats," he said, "that the conventions of courtly love are still thriving here in Italy?"

"No, I didn't," Keats replied with some wry humour. And I laughed softly, for there hadn't seemed anything courtly or proper about how Byron and those girls had responded to each other.

"It is true. They call it serventismo. A lady may be loved by her acknowledged amico, her cavalier, and her husband must accept it. Indeed, if the lover is an English lord, one might even suppose the husband is flattered by the attentions paid to his wife."

I was gaping in shock, and Keats was, too. "My lord," he murmured in protest.

"Of course, the affair is supposed to be strictly platonic," Byron added airily. And he favoured us with a broad wink.

"Of course."

"And so," Byron concluded, "I am in servitude to La Guiccioli… sweet Teresa… and I am expected to remain faithful." He sighed. "In some respects, it is *far* worse than being a husband!"

Once we reached Byron's rooms, I retired to a quiet corner with the Vico manuscript, while Keats sat back on a sofa, resting his head. "Make yourself comfortable," Byron murmured. It was clear that Keats was tired. "Are you quite well?"

"Well enough, my lord," he replied sincerely. But Keats went so far as to lie back on the sofa, with his feet still resting awkwardly on the floor.

Byron went further still: he lifted one of Keats' feet, slid his shoe off, and placed it on the sofa, then did the same with its companion. It seemed that his lordship was capable of great kindness. "Is that better?"

"Yes, my lord," Keats said with a soft smile. And he turned a little onto his side, and settled himself; I knew he was at his most comfortable in that position, from watching him sleep on the sofa in our rooms.

"Then do not stir yourself. Let me entertain you instead." Byron went to fetch a volume from his collection. He sat in a chair beside Keats, crossed one leg over the other, and leafed through the book to find a specific page. "Here we are…" And he began reciting in a quietly captivating voice: "*Ripe was the drowsy hour; the blissful cloud of summer-indolence benumb'd my eyes; my pulse grew less and less; pain had no sting, and pleasure's wreath no flower…*"

Keats chuckled delightedly. "You read very well, my lord."

"I am glad of it. *The last, whom I love more, the more of blame is heap'd upon her, maiden most unmeek – I knew to be my demon Poesy.* Your demon, John? Can I perhaps go so far as to suggest she is your demon lover?"

"Perhaps…"

"And yet – *No, she has not a joy – at least for me – so sweet as drowsy noons, and evenings steep'd in honied indolence…*"

"Ah, but I forgot the joy to be had by finding one's own words in another man's mouth."

A charged silence ensued. I looked up, knowing what I'd find: Byron staring rapt at my friend where he lay with his eyes closed. Keats seemed utterly relaxed and yet utterly vulnerable.

"We should weave you a garland," said Byron, "such as graced Alcibiades at the symposium, a garland of ivy and violets and ribbons."

"I do like violets," Keats murmured.

"It would look very well on you." After a moment, Byron stirred, but only to fetch another volume. "Let's try this… *His body was as straight as Circe's wand; Jove might have sipped out nectar from his hand. Even as delicious meat is to the taste, so was his neck in touching… I could tell ye how smooth his breast was, and how white his belly, and whose immortal fingers did imprint that heavenly path with many a curious dint that runs along his back…"*

"Marlowe's *Amorous Leander, beautiful and young.*"

"Just so. He almost intrigues one into following those curious dints down such a heavenly path – to wherever it might lead."

Keats laughed. "Well, I do say that a poet should be a chameleon, as Shakespeare must have been."

"Indeed," Byron said in low tones, "Shakespeare must have been many things to many people. What do you think he was to Kit Marlowe?"

"Who can say, my lord?"

"And you, John…"

"*I*, my lord?" Keats replied in amusement. I only realised how deep was my unease when I had the relief of hearing Keats' clear response: "Oh, I am getting far too old now to be the object of any man's fancy. And, chameleonic though I try to be, it takes a *great* deal of poetry to convince me that I might fancy boys. The scruffy exuberant conniving little ragamuffins are quite safe from me."

"But you are thinking of the old model for such loves, of Apollo and Hyacinthus, the lover and the beloved. I am thinking of the new model, of the love of heroes, of Achilles and Patroclus, Shakespeare and Marlowe, the love between equals – *the sacred communion of thighs.*"

"I am no hero, my lord. And the world says I am not your equal."

"I say you are, John, both hero and equal."

Keats gave a gusty sigh. "This is unexpected praise…"

"Is it so? When I have already admired your fine figure? I know, I know – you will protest that you are too short, and I will counter that you are perfectly formed. Exquisitely so. And I will add… that I may be tall, and I may have a good profile, but I am *not* perfectly formed…"

A silence ensued. Byron walked with the slightest limp, at never more than a stately pace, and I had heard that he'd been born with some deformity in one foot. It was hardly something I ever expected to hear him talk of. I wondered if Keats' sympathy would be touched, and do the work that his vanity hadn't.

"You honour me, my lord. I am greatly honoured, and I am also humbled by the trust you place in me. Nevertheless…" Keats opened his eyes and tilted his head back to look at Byron very directly, conveying his sincerity. I was sitting there adding my own will power to my friend's: *He's saying no.*

Byron sighed a little, and then sat up straighter. Reached for one of the volumes piled next to his chair. He said, "Let's read some Shakespeare. What will you have?"

"*King Lear*," was the instant reply.

So *King Lear* it was. "*I thought the king had more affected the Duke of Albany than Cornwall…*"

Christmas Day

A week passed. I made no progress in my task, and I felt abysmally low about it.

I saw little of the others. Shelley and Mary were taking care of little Percy, who was suffering some minor ailment; they were quite understandably concerned about the health of their only surviving child. Severn was busy either looking after Keats and our lodgings, or preparing to paint his *Death of Alcibiades*. I don't think Severn was aware of his tuneless humming as he worked on one thing or another, but it meant he was happy, and as such it did on occasion lift my own spirits. Keats spent his time resting or reading, and occasionally making notes for his poem on Sabrina, defender of female chastity. Byron kept his distance. I assumed he had been embarrassed to not only have attempted the seduction of my friend with a witness present, but to have been rejected, no matter how respectfully.

Meanwhile, I followed Hart when I could, and if not him then the cardinal. But I learned nothing new. Keats dissuaded me from approaching the cardinal, and anyway Mary said that his English was as bad as my Italian. It was incredibly frustrating. I should have written Captain Mitchell a letter, but I couldn't bear to report my failings. I owed him more than this. I owed my Lady Elena.

A week passed, and Christmas Day dawned. It promised to be grim rather than festive; even grimmer than those I'd spent at sea, though the situation was very similar, with our home and our families so far away.

The situation was also similar in that I was with friends. We each had a gift for the other two, though we had not agreed to do so. For Severn, I had found an engraving of a bust of Alcibiades that he had admired in the Vatican galleries. For Keats, a volume of Dante that Byron pointed out to me while we browsed a bookshop just off the Corso. Severn's gift to me was more practical, and gratefully received: a more comfortable bedroll for my place on the floor. Keats had gone to the trouble of having Byron's Vico manuscript copied for me. I said my thanks as eloquently as a sailor might hope to, and tried to convey my certainty that if I achieved nothing else in Italy I could not be dissatisfied, as I had found true friendship and affection.

Letters arrived. Keats was delighted to receive one from Charles Brown, his closest friend in England. But when he opened it, another letter fell out onto his lap; it must have been enclosed with Brown's. He picked it up, and read the direction. Realised who had sent it. And his face fell into despair.

"What is it?" I asked. "Bad news?" Though he hadn't even read either letter yet. Severn was looking worried, sorrowful, compassionate. He understood.

"No," said Keats, his voice cracking. "I trust not." Then he cried, "I can hardly bear to see her handwriting!"

"John," murmured Severn.

"It is from Fanny." Keats looked up at me. "Miss Brawne. The young woman I mentioned to you."

"Yes."

"I cannot stand this!"

Which was confusing. I would have thought he'd be elated. "But if she is writing to you, then she is keeping the faith. She is waiting for you. Unless you think –" I couldn't say it. *Unless you think this letter announces she is breaking with you.* But I did not see why any young woman would break with John Keats.

"I will never see her again," Keats said in a strangely pitched, monotonous tone. "I will die here, and I will never see her, or hear her, or touch her. Not in this life, and there will be no other life beyond, not for me. I will never have her. And the lack is killing me."

Severn remained silent, but I was deeply moved to argue. "You are getting better, John! You are not wholly well yet, I grant you, but you are so much better now than when first we met. Once your health has returned, you can go home again, and marry her, and she will be yours."

He looked up at me then as if I were torturing him. "I cannot hope for it."

"Why not? Tell me! *Why not?*"

"You speak of hope as if it were a good thing."

"It is!"

"When I feel hope, it is like a knife through my heart."

I glanced in appeal at Severn, but it seemed he had no comfort to offer – or none that had not already been rejected, perhaps. He hovered, but kept out of the way. I demanded angrily, "How can you speak so, when hope comes from God?"

"I'm sorry, Andrew, but I cannot believe in the Christian God. I'm sorry, Joseph."

"Well, that is an argument for another day." I was pacing back and forth across the small sitting room, unwontedly furious. "I am sure you believe in the virtues of faith, hope and charity. You personify faith and charitable love every day. Why not hope? Why not hope *for yourself?* Do you have any reason to doubt Miss Brawne?"

"No. No, I –" Pain spasmed across his face. "Andrew, I am not proud of myself. At my worst, I am a jealous cur. I have plagued Fanny with my jealousies and insecurities."

"And yet she is brave, and she keeps the faith."

He nodded, but shakily as if it cost him to do so. "Yes. I have come to know that. I know it – intellectually, as it were. And yet… here I am writing a prayer to Sabrina. Defender, as Byron reminds us, of female chastity. I am all too aware that the issue… continues to concern me."

I kept pacing back and forth, arguing within myself. But I knew I had forced my friend to be as open and vulnerable as he could possibly be. And I did not want to hurt him in such a state.

Eventually Keats asked, "Andrew, why does this concern *you* so closely?"

It was a good question, and a fair one. "I want you to get better," I said. And I finally made myself stop. I stood at the window, and looked blindly out across the piazza. "I want you to regain your health. And yet how can you ever be fully healed when you have no hope? You are blighting your own chances of recovery."

He murmured an assent, at least of understanding.

"Of course," I added, "once you are better, I want you to return to England and claim your love. Something I can never do now, and could never have done before. It is a foolish notion," I confessed in low tones, "but it would make it easier to bear my loss, if I knew you had not lost as well."

"It is not foolish, Andrew," he said softly. "I will try harder. To hope. To have faith in the future."

I turned back to face him. Severn was watching us. Of course he had not been told the details, but I was sure he understood my situation now, or guessed.

Keats held Miss Brawne's letter out to me. "I *will* try, I promise. However, I cannot bear to read this yet. Will you keep it safe for me? Until I ask for it."

I reached to take it, though I frowned. "Will you not keep it yourself?"

"Not yet. But do you understand? Andrew, you must keep it safe. *This is my soul on paper.* You must not let Iago take it, as he has stolen so much else."

I gaped at him, dimly aware of a whole dizzying range of meaning opening up before me. I hardly dared think. I simply took the letter, and slipped it away into the pocket over my heart. This was Keats' soul in my keeping.

We had all been invited to Byron's rooms for Christmas dinner. The seven of us sat around a large round table, including Fletcher who Mary asked to sit beside her. It was one of the freedoms accorded to exiles, I supposed, that the servant might mix with the master and his friends. Fletcher seemed easy enough, but he remained withdrawn in such situations, and did not impose his presence on the gathering. And if anything needed fetching or sorting, he was always first to his feet.

Once we finished our roast beef, Keats lifted his glass of dark red claret and proposed a toast. "Normally I would drink to Apollo, god of healing and of poetry. Long may he smile upon us all! But in honour of this fine claret provided by our most generous host, I will drink to Dionysius, god of freedom, ecstasy and wine!"

Of course no one could resist such a toast. We downed our glasses, and the bottle was passed around again.

"Apollo and Dionysius are both beautiful in their different ways," Byron opined, "but I must give Dionysius the edge. He is the best of man and the best of woman, combined in one. A truly intoxicating mix!"

"There is a statue in the Palazzo Borghese," Shelley confessed. "Perhaps you've seen it. When we were here in Rome last, I found it endlessly fascinating." His cheeks were glowing red, whether with wine or embarrassment. "It is called *The Sleeping Hermaphrodite*. It is quite the most beautiful thing I ever saw."

An edgy silence fell, and no one dared to quite meet anyone else's eyes, especially not Mary's. But then Severn spluttered into laughter, Byron roared after him, and soon we were all chuckling away quite merrily. Even Fletcher couldn't hide a smirk, despite the impatient roll of his eyes, as if to say, *Poets! Forever inappropriate, but what can you expect?*

"You know," said Byron once we had all calmed down again. "You know –" His gaze remained on the tablecloth, as if even Byron were a little ashamed of what he was about to say. "Our own Iago is beautiful in much the same way."

Silence. I sat there, turned to forbidding stone.

"A man with the best of womankind in him; he embodies every kind of beauty. And fascinating. Endlessly fascinating."

Silence. No one approved of this. Or at least, no one was comfortable.

"He tells the most wonderful stories… A kind of modern-day Scheherazade."

God, what had been going on this past week? I felt as if everyone was waiting on me to react, but it was Fletcher who spoke. "My lord," he said heavily, "why don't you tell your friends what you intend?"

Byron glared at him. "You forget yourself, man."

"I am not the one forgetting myself," he stubbornly replied.

"What?" I demanded, hard as fate. "What have you done?"

"Nothing! Nothing yet."

I wasn't going to let him out of this one. "What do you *intend* to do?"

Byron gave a languid shrug. "I intend to move to the Palazzo Amara tomorrow. Mr Hart has need of a companion. As do I."

There was the briefest moment of shocked silence, before the entire table erupted into gasps and exclamations.

"What?" I cried, my hands curled into fists. The arrogance, the audacity, the *stupidity…*

"What is the *matter* with you?" Severn demanded. His uncharacteristic outburst momentarily startled Byron, but then he merely waved a dismissive hand.

Mary said only, "Byron." Her disapproval was clear, as was Fletcher's and Keats'. Fletcher had been standing there solidly with his arms crossed, and Keats was shaking his head. I was simply horrified.

"I am tired of living in hotels," Byron complained, as if this were reason enough.

"Lodgings," Shelley said in a strangled tone. "Mary and I will share lodgings with you, if you don't want to live alone."

Byron looked at him with greater pleading than I had ever thought to see on his face. "Shiloh my dear, you will understand. I will be able to recover your letters for you. And Sullivan," he said, turning to me. "I will be able to discover more information. Maybe find those papers of yours. Just as you recovered Severn's sketch."

"Why? If Hart is to be your companion, why would you act against him?"

"Because you are my friends."

I shook my head. "You are no friend of mine, my lord. Hart is my sworn enemy. He is the enemy of Captain Sir William Mitchell, and the enemy of England."

"Hart is a gentleman," Byron was stung into retorting.

I pushed back my chair and stood. I was furious, but I knew exactly what I was doing. I was offering an insult that could only be answered by blood. "What do *you* know of gentlemen? Always pledging yourself to the wrong person. You boast of making love to another man's wife, and you call it courtly! And now you would be companion to someone who has caused the greatest harm to those who have far more merit than you."

Byron snorted. He also stood, restless with anger. I half expected him to fight me then and there, but instead he paced away. "So he has given Lord C— a scare. I call that justice."

"Even if you would dismiss that, you know it is not the only charge against Hart."

"You and your captain have had your differences with the man, but I cannot believe he is so bad as all that. Have you ever spoken with him at length?"

"No. I've never even met him."

"Then you don't know what he is."

"I know very well what he is! It's you who's been blinded. Seduced by beauty, so that you cannot see the truth."

He let out a ringing laugh. "Oh, you are a fine one to lecture me about morals."

"I know when I can act upon an urge, and when I cannot. I know what is natural, and what is not."

"What is unnatural is how you tie yourself up in knots, trying to be pure and righteous."

"I'd rather that than be impure," I muttered. I looked around at the others. To my surprise, no one was taking sides. Byron must mean far more to them all than I did, as so new an acquaintance – but then no one seemed happy that Byron was throwing in his lot with Hart.

I turned away. There was no point in arguing with Byron, was there? Neither of us would ever convince the other.

But to have one of our friends becoming companion to Hart… And perhaps more than companion, from what I knew of Byron's inclinations. Was the man so desperately lonely? I cast an anguished glance at Keats, who looked back at me with concern. If I had known what Byron would be driven to, I would almost have preferred that Keats had let himself be seduced. At least then we would not have lost an ally.

Perhaps he could even now be regained, if I told the whole truth. It wasn't too late, was it? I knew nothing of what had passed since I was last in these rooms, willing Byron to accept Keats' refusal, but it wasn't too late if Byron had yet to move to the palazzo. Actually, the one thing I did know now was that Byron had been seduced in part by stories. And I had one of my own.

I returned to the table, and stood with my hands on the back of my chair. The others waited to hear what I would say. And I spoke in the most reasonable tones I could manage. "Can you not understand how much I hate this man, and with reason? Lady Elena – she was not a prig, but she was *pure*. I realise you do not value purity, my lord, but Elena was *happy*. I have found that to be rare in this world. Rare and precious. She loved her husband, and he adored her. She was the best woman, the best *person*, I ever met with."

I looked around at my friends. Everyone was rapt. Even Lord Byron. I continued in a harder tone: "Adrian Hart caused her to feel such shame that she killed herself. This man who was supposedly her own brother, her only remaining family. He destroyed the peace of mind of the person who most deserved peace."

At this, Mary leaned towards me in concern, as if she wanted to comfort me. Fletcher put his head down so that I could not see his face. Severn was blushing a little. The others, with raised eyebrows or parted mouths, indicated their sympathetic interest. Byron in particular seemed intrigued.

"Shame?" Shelley asked, very carefully. "Are you saying there was something beyond the theft of the papers…?"

The horror of it possessed me again, and I, too, felt unutterable shame. "Perhaps. There was something more. He did something… This was never made clear to me."

I felt as if I had betrayed her, even in saying thus much, for I guessed what conclusions they would leap to. And they were indeed fascinated; I knew all too well that an unnatural love between brother and sister was a frequent topic of poetry. In life, it merely brought squalor and disgrace; the sinners were quite literally deprived of God's grace.

I rounded on them fiercely, "If God is just and merciful, then Elena is in heaven, for no blame could attach to her character or her intentions. No matter what occurred, all the shame of it belongs to *him*."

"Of course," they murmured. "Of course."

"I am sure her heart remained pure," Byron murmured, though he seemed too distracted to be actually offering me comfort. "God will forgive her for any excessive generosity towards those she had reason to love."

Keats tentatively asked, "But why do you say he was *supposedly* her brother? Is there some doubt of the family connection?"

"No. No. Only, I cannot bring myself to believe that anyone so closely connected with her could have used her so cruelly."

We went our separate ways not long after. But before we parted, I offered a tentative apology. "What I have said is true," I quietly declared, "and I will stand by it. But I should not have argued so with our host, who has been so kind as to take us in. Not on such a day, and on such a festive occasion."

Keats smiled at me, and shook my hand. "What else is Christmas for, my friend?"

I shook everyone's hand, including Mary's. Including Byron's. He met my gaze, looking troubled and a little shamed. I did not know if I had made him change his mind, but I had at least made my point.

And thus we parted.

It had been a difficult and turbulent day, and I had not had much chance to think. But as I lay on my new bedroll that night, I remembered what Keats had said that morning. It seemed a year ago.

He had handed me the letter from Miss Brawne. And he had said, *This is my soul on paper. Do not let Iago steal it.*

Bleakness

Fletcher could not meet with me until the Wednesday, the day after Boxing Day. I bought him a birra at a trattoria just off the Via del Babuino. We sat in silence for a while, as we eased back into our former feeling of companionship. Once we'd downed the beers, I bought a second round.

Then, before Fletcher could speak, I warned him: "I cannot trust your master any longer. I can no longer consider him a friend."

Fletcher shrugged, indicating his acceptance of what must be. "I know that, sir. And I do not blame you. But he's committed to Mr Hart now. I like it little better than you do, but there it is."

"Do you know what Hart is?"

"He always behaves like a perfect gentleman, Mr Sullivan, and he is more courteous to me than most." Fletcher frowned, and tipped his head for a moment's consideration. "But I have no reason to doubt what you tell us of him."

"Would you… Could you meet with me on occasion, do you think, and pass on any information you discover? Only about Hart, not about Byron. Or am I asking too much?"

"Well, you aren't," Fletcher said slowly, "for his lordship swears to me that he will do the same. He says he will still meet with you all, and he will tell you what he can. And he hasn't said I shouldn't. So for now I will follow his lead."

I stared at him. "That's a dangerous game your master is playing."

"How so, sir?"

"Call me Andrew, for God's sake. Or at least Sullivan."

"Yes, sir. But tell me how it's dangerous. You never said Mr Hart was a violent man."

"No, but he creates such despair in people that they take their own lives."

Fletcher's mouth quirked for a moment, and his eyes glinted. Then he caught me glaring at this moment of wholly inappropriate amusement. "Beg pardon, Mr Sullivan. Mr Hart has caused much grief, that is true. But I think my master is safe."

"How so?"

"His lordship would not do the world such a disservice as to remove himself from it before his time."

"I see," I said. And I could almost share the humour. "Nevertheless, I assume you would not claim that he is not open to blackmail or coercion."

Fletcher, naturally enough, did not comment. Despite his public disagreements with his master, Fletcher struck me as the most loyal of men. Perhaps because his occasional blunt challenges always seemed to have Byron's best interests at heart.

"You *must* go with him, I suppose?"

"Yes, sir."

"You put yourself in danger, too."

Fletcher shrugged. "There is no help for that. Anyway, I am a stubborn old creature, and I only do what I know is right. I am not afraid of being judged, so Hart can have nothing over me."

"He could twist your loyalty to Byron."

"Could he, sir? Well, loyalty is a fine thing in itself. And I will not condemn my master for it." Fletcher took a breath. Looked around him. Then he leaned closer to me and said in low, urgent tones, "His lordship says he never loves, but that's not true. And when he does love, whether it's a friend or a romance, it is with his whole heart. There's no help for it, sir." He sat back again. "That's the way things are."

"You can't think that Hart deserves Byron's faith?"

"No, sir. That library full of papers. I had a proper look for myself. There's proof enough of his bad intent."

I shook my head, trying to understand. "And Byron has broken faith with the rest of us. With Shelley, his oldest friend here. Loyalty may be a fine thing, but not when it's compromised. Not where there are conflicts between an old loyalty and a new one."

"He wouldn't let Hart do the rest of you any harm."

"But, Fletcher –" I stopped. I had thought I understood Fletcher, and that he and I were more alike than not. But for now I was just confused. I sat back. Then I asked for the sake of clarification, "You are still willing to tell me things about Hart?"

"Yes, sir."

"All right." There was one thing I'd remained unsatisfied about, despite all my spying. "Byron said he couldn't remember any servants at the palazzo, and I've never seen any. What can you tell me of that?"

Fletcher nodded. "There are a couple of servants, sir. Wizened old things. A married couple, as far as I can tell, and a bit odd. I don't see them about much, but things get done. I don't understand them at all. But they're Italian, so maybe that's just how it is."

"Thank you, Fletcher."

The man examined his pocket watch. "I'd better be on my way, sir. I will see you at the service on Sunday?"

"Yes. Thank you."

And I sat there alone in the trattoria over another beer. Pondering the nature of Byron's relationship to Hart, and that of Fletcher's to Byron. Despite Fletcher's proud stubborn righteousness, I was worried for him. Though I could not yet see just how Hart would gain a hold over him, other than through his loyalty to Byron.

Byron himself was an easier matter for Hart to pin down: a letter, whether affectionate or loving, that was all it would take. A poem addressed to his new companion, perhaps confessing more than he ought. And there would be another document to add to the piles in the library at the palazzo.

Then I ruefully reflected that Hart had stolen Byron himself now, so what need did he have of Byron's soul on paper?

Relief

I finally received a letter from Captain Mitchell, and discovered that he had been ordered to take the *Boadicea* out of Naples. I hadn't received a response to either of my last two letters, which themselves had been delayed in the sending, and which had both reported my utter lack of progress. It had been so long that I had feared – no, I had *known* that my captain was vastly disappointed with me.

The reality turned out to be that the *Boadicea* was on a run to Gibraltar, and my captain was pleased enough with me to be explicitly reassuring. *Of course,* he wrote, *if Hart is living as a law-abiding gentleman, then we cannot move against him. To do so would make us no better than him. Wait. Be patient. He will show his hand again soon enough.* Captain Mitchell also advised that he had transferred more money into the account he'd given me access to, given that my stay in Rome was proving of longer duration than we'd anticipated.

I was not only deeply relieved, but strangely reinvigorated. I continued my surveillance of both Hart and the cardinal, when I could. I also commissioned Severn to sketch a series of street scenes on the Corso, keeping an eye on the Palazzo Amara while he did so. But I also ensured I made the time to accompany Keats on a walk on the Pincian Hill each afternoon, and I contributed more effort and resources towards the food we three ate. Keeping John Keats in good health must be a priority as important as working against Adrian Hart.

One afternoon, as Keats and I were walking across the Piazza del Popolo, I was surprised to see a young man on the steps of the Palazzo Amara. Usually from the street the place seemed shut up and deserted. As we drew closer, I saw the fellow was young, perhaps not even twenty; strong and handsome. From the way he was dressed, I assumed he was a labourer of some kind, but still there was something about him which indicated a cleverness, an education, a sensitivity. He was pounding at the front door of the palazzo, and calling out in great frustration.

"Do you understand him?" Keats asked as we walked slowly by. We were curious, of course, but we didn't have to hide it, as most of the passersby looked at the young man inquisitively.

"No. But I'm sure he called the name *Iago*. And it sounds like he wants to be let in."

"I wonder if Iago's at home." For there was no answer from within the palazzo. "I wonder if Byron's there. He, at least, would be used to ignoring the importunate knockings of his creditors." When Keats saw me trying not to laugh at the expense of our erstwhile friend, he muttered, "Sorry."

We reached Severn, who was sketching on the corner of the Corso and the Via Condotti, looking back towards the north. "You passed our young visitor," he observed.

"Yes."

"He came this morning, as well. I am sure Iago is at home, but there's been no response at all. I wonder what he wants."

"And why won't Iago see him?" Keats added.

We loitered for a while, until the young fellow finally gave up and strode off angrily with his head down, leaving us none the wiser.

Byron had invited us all to a late dinner on the eve of the new year, at a restaurant near Shelley and Mary's hotel. I had to assume that the choice of a public venue was due in part to the wish to avoid another loud argument between Byron and me, so I went with the intention of remaining on my best behaviour.

I had already spoken with Fletcher that day, when Severn and I had met him at the usual church service. Mary had joined us as well, bringing her little son who seemed fully recovered from his illness. Fletcher had very little news to pass on. When I asked him about the young man who'd been trying to gain entrance to the Palazzo Amara, Fletcher shrugged. "I don't know who he is, sir, but I gather he had hopes of becoming Mr Hart's companion. Before his lordship took the post."

For the sake of peace, I resolved not to ask Byron anything about Hart, nor even raise the topic. This resolution was made easier by the fact that I hardly wanted to talk to the man. I still felt angry over his betrayal of us.

When Byron arrived, he was obviously feeling embarrassed and somewhat guilty. But it was quite provoking to see that, beneath his consciousness of wrong-doing, Byron was also deeply content. His current situation suited him, and he only seemed confused by the fact that he knew his friends could not approve.

All was polite, and the conversation was safe. Until at last Byron himself began. He cleared his throat, and then announced, "I have been looking for your letters, Shelley."

We all fell quiet and looked at him, as there had been no attempt to address Shelley in confidence. Only Shelley kept his head low, sitting back and looking down at the table.

"Whenever I have had the chance. I have been searching through that room. I probably have as little hope as Sisyphus of completing the task, but I am trying."

"Thank you," Shelley said. We all left a respectful and no doubt a curious silence. But then, eventually, Shelley spoke again, as quietly as if he were in a confessional. "There were a lot of letters in that box. A lot of evils. I know that I have done great harm."

"Come, Shiloh," Byron murmured. "You are no worse than most men, and a great deal better than many."

He shook his head. "I have been thinking on those letters. There were some from a Miss Hitchener. She lived as my sister for a while, with me and Harriet. My first wife," he explained. "But we had to break with her. And… she was alone in the world, she relied on making her way as a teacher. Nothing improper ever passed between us, but her reputation had suffered."

"You gave her money to live on," Byron reminded him.

"It would have been better not to get into the situation in the first place."

"We live and we learn."

"I find this life most difficult," Shelley said in a strained tone, "when I follow my ideals. For inevitably the world demands quite the opposite. Or I should say that *society demands*, for my ideals are as much a part of the world as society's rules are. And I cannot yet think I am wrong. Only that, in the end, I am forced to compromise. Society will not bend so far."

Byron sighed. "And so here we are in exile, all of us."

I wanted to say, *Speak for yourself.* For Keats and Severn and I could still call England our home, and surely Fletcher and Mary could, too.

Mary offered to her husband, "You always do what you think is best. That takes courage, and I love you for it."

And he took her hand in both of his, and he smiled. It was a wan smile, but a genuine.

Byron left us again in the early evening, announcing that he must prepare for attending a masked ball. Fletcher of course must go with him, to assist. The Shelleys returned to their hotel.

And so Severn and I took Keats home. Fletcher joined us later, when he could. And the four of us saw in the new year with the best bottle of claret we could afford.

Eve and the Serpent – January 1821

On New Year's Day I was walking across the Piazza del Popolo when I saw a young man drinking, alone and disconsolate. It was the fellow who'd demanded entry to the Palazzo Amara and been denied. Worse than that, I suppose, he'd been ignored.

He was sitting outside a trattoria despite the cold weather, his strong body sprawled heedlessly on a chair. A large carafe of white wine waited on the table, near at hand; it was already half gone. I couldn't quite pin him down, for while he had the healthy bulk of a labourer, his clothes were of good quality, though old and worn and currently covered in dust as if he'd walked a long road. And even his brooding expression had an intelligent edge.

For a moment or two, I held my course. But then I decided to approach him. "Buon giorno," I offered in what was no doubt a pitiful accent.

It seemed to take a while for him to register my presence, but eventually he looked up. He frowned briefly at me, glanced over his shoulder at the palazzo, just visible down the Corso, and then returned to his introspection.

I had very little Italian even now, so I tried, "Parla inglese?"

He just shook his head dismissively. I didn't blame him.

I decided to give it one last try, and ask if he was acquainted with Hart. Indicating the palazzo, I asked, "Conoscente Iago?"

That got his attention. He gazed up at me, eyes ablaze. Then he was on his feet, and he was talking, talking, so fast and so angrily I had no hope at all of understanding him. Advancing on me, gesturing strongly. I took a step back. Then he flung his arm out, pointing, demanding. It was perfectly clear he was telling me to go away.

I lifted my hands placatingly. "I have no quarrel with you," I said, hoping he'd understand my intent if not my words. "I just wanted to talk with you. Offer my help if you needed it."

Again a torrent of Italian words, Italian gestures, which needed no translating.

"Scuze," I offered with a bow, and I walked away.

When they didn't go out, Byron and Hart would spend the evening quietly, reading books and newspapers, or talking together for hours at a time, listening enthralled to each other's stories. Then Byron would often stay up half the night writing; Hart either retired or kept him company while reading a book. I knew all this because I watched them.

On each of those evenings, I followed the route Fletcher and I had taken once before. I used a ladder to climb over a wall into the courtyard neighbouring the Palazzo Amara, and used barrels, wooden crates, or whatever was to hand to clamber up the palazzo's garden wall. Then I sat there on top of the wall, amongst the bare branches of one of the trees. The two men would sit together in a long room across the back of the palazzo, with floor length windows, lit by firelight and by more candles and lamps than I could afford to use in a year.

I was sure they wouldn't ever see me, as their eyes could not possibly adjust to the darkness outside while they were cocooned within that bright glow. On three different evenings, however, Hart had gazed out of the window directly at me, his eyes focused at exactly the right distance. It was eerie and unsettling, and I would freeze in place, hardly daring to breathe in case he spied the white puffs of warm air from my lips or even saw my chest rise and fall. Yet it must have been a coincidence. There was no way he could have seen me.

A week to the day after Byron moved to the Palazzo Amara, Mary went to visit him there, to see if her old friend was happy in his new home. And it seemed he was, for he was in mischievously high spirits.

She came to our lodgings afterwards to report back to me and Keats – Severn was out at the time. "Iago was there when I arrived," Mary said. "He was very urbane; welcomed me with the utmost courtesy. He even complimented me on *Frankenstein*, though he wouldn't tell me how he knew it was mine. Byron said he hadn't told him."

This was wonderful enough news to shake me from my preoccupation with Hart. I remembered that the novel had been published anonymously. "Then I must compliment you, too, my lady," I said. "I read that tale with equal amounts of terror and pleasure – a great deal of each. And it stayed on my mind for such a long time afterwards."

"Thank you," she said, bestowing on me an uncomplicatedly happy smile. Then she did me the kindness of reverting to the topic I was most interested in. "So, your Mr Hart. As he was being so friendly, I asked him why he was calling himself Iago."

I was stunned. Perhaps Mary Shelley knew no fear. "What did he reply?"

"He just laughed, and quoted the play: *I am not what I am.*"

This actually sent a shudder down my spine. I, who had been in battle a dozen times, who had held a man down while our surgeon amputated his arm – I, who had seen my lady laid in the ground – I shuddered at these words. "What did he mean?"

She shook her head. "I can only think of the obvious: that he is hiding something. That there is some question of his true identity."

"But he is Lady Elena's brother. He is accepted in society as a gentleman. He doesn't have an occupation. What else could he possibly be than what he is?"

"I don't know. But I'll try to find out, if you like."

"You'll be visiting the palazzo again?"

"Yes." She considered me for a long moment. "You mustn't think we're all befriending this man and deserting you. I really only want to see Byron. This afternoon, Mr Hart left the place not ten minutes after I'd arrived. Byron – Byron can be very entertaining when he wants to be. When he hasn't already infuriated you. As you may remember."

"Yes," I admitted. "I do." It belatedly occurred to me than that Byron mustn't be too awful a person if Mary was still fond of him. She, if anyone, had cause to be disillusioned. I had gathered from overhearing various conversations between Byron and Shelley that the 'Miss Claire' who Byron occasionally referred to in dismissive tones was Mary's stepsister, who had had a child by Byron and been abandoned. Apart from which, Mary herself had been married for years to a radical and a poet and an exile, and I gathered her life hadn't been made easier by her marriage – so she would hardly idealise the type. And yet she still loved and liked Byron, and could be charmed by him.

"He was in a fine mood. He took my hand and led me to the library. It's staggering, isn't it? Mr Hart's collection of papers. Despite all of your descriptions, I hadn't comprehended quite how vast it is." She smiled a little, then. "But it was the books that impressed me. I realise that can't be his own collection; it must belong to the palazzo. What an astonishing variety! Every area of knowledge or art represented. And so many first editions, of the highest significance. I was quite dazzled."

Keats murmured, "Now you have me yearning to go there myself."

Mary laughed. "I'm sorry, John. *You* must be the one to remain standing firm by Mr Sullivan, I'm afraid."

He accepted this with a good grace.

"But there was something quite strange… Byron showed me the shelf which held all the works of my parents – Mary Wollstonecraft and William Godwin," she added for my benefit. "First editions in English, and a few translations. A bound collection of their essays. I haven't seen all the volumes together like that outside of my own family home. I took them down and browsed through them."

Keats was smiling gently. "I'm glad you had that joy, Mary."

"Thank you. Thank you. But the strange thing is – I had moved an object in order to reach the books. And eventually Byron picked it up and held it towards me. He said, *This wasn't here when last I saw these books. It must be for you.* And when I looked at it, it was an enamelled wooden apple. It was very beautiful. Perfect, and seductive. Part of me wanted to reach for it, and – well, if I couldn't bite into it, then at least play with it awhile. And another part of me was afraid, and didn't want to even touch it. Eventually I told Byron to put it down."

I thought I already had the answer, but still I asked carefully, "What did that mean to you, my lady?"

Mary hesitated, so Keats supplied, "I can't think beyond Eve and the serpent and the Tree of Knowledge."

"Yes," she agreed. "In Eve's place, I probably would have done as she did. But I have long been interested in whether and how we consider the consequences of our actions and our inaction. How thoughtfully we decide."

"That's what *Frankenstein* is about," I said. "Is it not?"

"Yes. The heedless pursuit of knowledge is his downfall." She looked at each of us. "So that seemed strange to me, that this symbol of my own interests was there waiting for me with my parents' books – even though Mr Hart hadn't expected me to visit."

It was all I could do not to shudder again. "It's like me finding Severn's sketch under the Vico."

"Exactly."

And we all looked at each other with widened eyes, afraid that we were taking this a bit too seriously – and also afraid that we weren't taking it quite seriously enough.

Eros and Thanatos

It was Byron's thirty-third birthday on the twenty-second of January. Mary went to visit him after an early dinner, but none of the rest of us saw him. It seemed that Hart occupied him more and more.

Keats and I were on the homeward leg of our regular afternoon walk that day, when we saw an anxious knot of people gathering on the steps of the Palazzo Amara. We glanced at each other, and broke into a run. Pushed through to discover what everyone had been alarmed by.

Not one of our friends – that was my first thought, and relief came with it. But then I realised it was the young man lying there on Adrian Hart's front steps. The young man who'd apparently been acquainted with Hart, and had then been dismissed. Who'd pounded at that very door for re-admittance.

Someone turned him over, and almost everyone drew back with a hiss or a cry, crossing themselves. The hefty hilt of a dagger in his chest. He'd thrust it up into his heart from below his breastbone; he would have been dead before he hit the ground. Yet another suicide to credit to Hart's account. Somehow I had no doubt of that.

But Keats asked the crowd, "Did anyone see this? Did anyone see what happened?"

I looked up and saw Severn standing just beyond the far edge of the gathering. He looked pale and sickened. When I asked him the same question with a lifted brow, he just shook his head. *No.* And then he slowly turned and walked away.

"Did this poor fellow kill himself?" Keats asked in a lower tone. "Andrew, do you know if that's even possible from what you can see?"

"Yes, it is. I can hardly think of a more efficient or effective method. He would have hardly known a thing." I closed my eyes, suddenly unable to look any more. Elena had been just as efficient, and even kinder to herself. An overdose of laudanum. She would have simply fallen asleep. *My lady... My own dear lady...*

Either the sky was threatening rain or my eyes were threatening tears of grief, frustration, rage. I turned, and pushed back through the crowd. Began striding down the Corso.

Keats jogged to catch up. "Andrew, wait. Unless you don't want company?"

I slowed down a little. "Your company is always welcome, John."

We walked along in silence for a while, until Keats tentatively asked, "Did you know him?"

"No. I tried to talk with him once. He was hurting too much to care. I never even knew his name." I sighed, and slowed down some more. "He interested me. He seemed a fine creature. Surprising. Perhaps I'm mistaken about who he was, or what he could have been. I don't know." And that was the problem, of course: "Now we'll never know."

"You weren't wrong to be interested," Keats offered in reply. "And you're certainly right about one thing: he was far too young to die."

I went to the palazzo that night, to see what could be seen from the garden wall. There was no bright glow in the long back room where Byron and Hart usually sat; it was lit only by the fire, and a very few candles. Byron was there alone – not reading, but haltingly pacing back and forth. He seemed restless, a little anxious. Every now and then he'd come to one of the long windows, and stare out at the night – but I don't think he could have seen anything at all, let alone me. Perhaps he stared in dissatisfaction at his own reflection.

As he continued alone and unsettled, I gave serious thought to climbing down into the garden, and talking with him. Perhaps he would be glad of a friendly word. Perhaps he wasn't as content with his situation as I'd thought. Perhaps he did not like that a man had killed himself on the palazzo's steps that very afternoon.

But of course I delayed too long, and just as I'd grasped a tree branch to start my climb down, Hart walked into the room.

Byron turned to him immediately, his anxiety increasing ten-fold. Hart was already saying something soothing, gesturing placatingly. And he didn't stop or keep his distance – he went right up to Byron, and rested his hands on Byron's arms. A brief exchange of words, and then a pause. Hart was softly smiling. Byron was staring at him, frowning, fraught. Yearning.

Then Hart pushed in closer, and met Byron's mouth with his own. And Hart was kissing him.

I had never seen two men kissing before, except in fraternity. Not with passion. Not with such affection. I just stared, not moving. Unable to move. Unable to think. Unsure whether, despite all my spying, I really wanted to know this.

The kiss broke, and the two embraced for a moment. Then Byron pulled away, shook his head, said something. Hart reassured him, and lifted his hands to push Byron's coat back off his shoulders so he was in shirtsleeves. Led Byron over to the sofa and sat him down. Knelt before him. Slipped off Byron's right shoe, slowly peeled off his stocking – and then lovingly lifted Byron's poor withered foot in both hands, and bent to press a kiss to it.

Byron was gazing at the man now with something far beyond affection. And I could not blame him for that. Even my breath had been stopped by this graceful generous gesture.

Still kneeling there on the floor, Hart drew close again, pushing between Byron's thighs – and Byron took him into his arms, and they were kissing once more. Ardently.

I retreated with as much care and discretion as I could manage.

I lay awake that night plagued with unwanted thoughts, unwonted imaginings. Not just of the unexpectedly passionate exchanges I had witnessed. But of… of something that had seemed very like love. It had stirred me, I could not deny that. And I wondered if…

I wondered if Hart had been even half so tender with Elena.

I found that I wished it were so.

'Why, this is Hell…'

Fletcher came to fetch us the next morning. "His lordship wants to talk with you all, if you will come. He is at Mr Shelley's hotel."

"A bit early for my lord, isn't it?" Severn tartly observed. It was barely past ten.

My heart sank, though I had been expecting this. "He has come to a decision, then."

"Yes, sir."

"He has committed himself to being Hart's companion. In the long term."

Fletcher looked at me oddly. "Quite the opposite, sir. Or so I am to understand. There was an arrangement made that I would go and fetch his belongings this afternoon while Mr Hart is out."

I stared at him for a moment, trying to take this in.

"Will you come, then?" Fletcher prompted me.

"Yes. Yes, of course!"

And there was a flurry of half-drunk tea being downed and coats being donned. Severn seemed uninterested, until Keats indicated with a tilt of the head that he should join us no matter how reluctant.

Minutes later we were walking into the Shelleys' sitting room at their hotel, and looking around curiously for Byron.

He was alone, and sitting slumped in an armchair in the dimmest corner of the room. Fletcher cast an impatient yet concerned glance at him, then retreated to a dining chair. Keats and Severn hovered uncertainly by the sofa. But I approached Byron, determined to see him clearly.

He was quiet and pale, anxiously brooding, his hands clasped together in his lap. He lifted his gaze to mine for a moment, but then dropped it again to the carpet. It was as if his very foundations had been rocked. "My lord," I ventured. "What has happened?"

A grimace, and now he would not meet my eyes. He was still pale, but the faintest colour appeared on his cheeks. He seemed a little humiliated.

"I cannot bear to tell this more than once. So let us wait for Shelley and Mary."

I felt utterly confused. Just when I had expected Byron to be content, happy, even overjoyed, he seemed badly shaken. And I felt sorry for him, for I had only just learned to feel more kindly towards Byron and his contrary nature. I waited there, still standing near Byron's chair.

At last Shelley came in, and then Mary. Fletcher stood, but Byron did not. "I'm sorry," Mary said. "Percy's been rather a handful this morning." She pulled a straight-backed chair closer to Byron, and reached to take his hand in hers. "Now, my dear friend, what is it you want to tell us?"

He looked at her helplessly, and then glanced around at the others. Shelley was sitting in an echoing slump on another armchair, while Keats and Severn had settled on the sofa. Finally Byron looked up at me where I still stood waiting.

And Byron announced, "I was half-joking before, calling that man Mephistopheles."

"Yes?" I said when Byron paused.

"Now I am serious. I am convinced on this. That man is the Devil incarnate."

Silence. I glanced around at the others, who were all staring at Byron in various states of uncertainty. No one seemed to know quite how to react, except perhaps for Severn, who was looking dismayed.

"What do you mean?" I asked. "Are you talking poetically? Metaphorically?"

"It is not a metaphor. It is the literal truth."

I was struggling with this. Only hours before I had been wrestling with the notion that Byron and Hart were capable of a genuine if illicit kind of love. Which I found to be a very earthly type of challenge. Now Byron wanted me to believe that Hart was actually the Devil. Which certainly made *the sacred communion of thighs* seem quite ordinary.

"But I don't understand," I continued, probably plaintive, certainly irritated. "Are you telling me that Adrian Hart never was Lady Elena's brother? Or that Hart has been possessed by some kind of devil?"

"Not *a* devil," Byron corrected me: "*the* Devil."

Severn slid off the sofa onto his knees and began praying. "*Our Father which art in heaven…*" Even Byron cast him an irritated look.

"I do not know the answer to your question," Byron continued. "But it does occur to me that if the Devil fancied walking the world for a while, then he could not have chosen a more beautiful vessel in which to do so."

Shelley scoffed. "Why should the Devil be walking the world?"

"Why should he not? Mephistopheles didn't even distinguish between the two: *Why, this is Hell, nor am I out of it.*"

"If this is already Hell, I am sure the Devil finds it incredibly tedious. What happened to the lake of unquenchable fire?"

"Maybe there is no Heaven or Hell, but only Hades," Byron parried. "And we are all already dead, wandering in a dull sort of half-life."

Of course they had lost me by now. None of this could be relevant.

Shelley was complaining, "The age of such visitations of devils and angels is long past, if indeed they were ever more than stories. Isn't it all too plain, in this modern age, that there is nothing beyond the everyday?"

"Can you *really* be so blind as to think that, Shelley?"

"I don't just think it, I *know* it. There is no such thing as the Devil, and Adrian Hart is not more nor less than a man, whether he fancies himself an Iago or not." Shelley glared at his friend. "And don't give me any of your *There are more things in heaven and earth, Horatio.*"

Finally they were both silent.

I cleared my throat. "My lord. Where is the proof of what you say?"

Byron cast me a disgruntled look. "I have no proof."

"Then, what is your reason for saying this? What happened to make you think this?"

Byron just shook his head. He couldn't or wouldn't explain. There was embarrassment in his air, but no doubt. It seemed he sincerely believed that Adrian Hart was the Devil.

I shook my head, remembering once more the tender gesture of Hart's as he blessed with a kiss that part of Byron that he considered the worst manifestation of himself. It had been the first time I'd thought well of Hart for so very long, and now that was all being completely undermined. Not that I *wanted* to think well of the man, but it had been such a relief to believe for one night at least that Elena's brother wasn't entirely evil. Except that now Byron was saying that actually he was. Entirely.

I had resisted for so long the notion that Byron's wayward inclinations could possibly be acceptable. And now, strangely, I was so convinced they were not only harmless but a positive good, that I could not believe an honest passion had so soon turned into such fear.

"Oh, but what *happened* last night?" I cried.

Byron stared at me with a mute refusal. I turned to Fletcher, who was the only other person who might know even as much I did. But he just shook his head, giving nothing away.

"All right," I said. "If Hart *is* the Devil, then what's he doing here? What is his purpose?"

"Isn't it obvious?" Byron said. "He's collecting souls."

"What?" Though I already knew instinctively what he meant.

"Each of those papers piled up in his library represents a soul."

Shelley, who could be supposed to have lost his soul along with his Pandora's Jar of letters, just laughed at this notion.

But I had already turned to Keats – who was staring at me with horror. My hand was already at my breast pocket. I drew out the letter from Miss Brawne, and showed it to him. His soul was still safe in my keeping. I offered it, but he lifted his hands, as if he still could not bear to even touch it. So I tucked it away again.

"My lord," said Keats after a moment, "what you say does actually accord with a feeling I'd had. If Iago wanted to steal anything from me, as he has stolen from Captain Mitchell and Shelley and Severn, then it would be that letter Andrew holds for me. But I still cannot quite think that Iago is *literally* stealing souls."

"He is a villain," Shelley averred. "Just an ordinary villain."

"And all those papers?" I asked.

Shelley shrugged. "Blackmail, or the threat of it. Learning secrets and putting them to use. Generally causing mischief."

"John," I said, "when you suggested Hart was Dionysius, you didn't mean it literally, did you?"

"No." He frowned, and thought for a long moment. "And yet the metaphor remains apt. Dionysius was also known as the Liberator, because he frees you from your ordinary self, he frees you from your cares and worries. He does that through madness or ecstasy or wine."

"But – the people he has stolen from – no one has felt *freed* by him. Instead they have felt oppressed!"

"Perhaps," Keats said very quietly – "perhaps we cling too close to our worldly cares. He might offer freedom by taking away our chains, but we might be too afraid to accept what he offers."

"No, I will not have it! He goes where he will, and leaves a turbulent wake behind in which people die. That young man took his own life. As did my poor lady. That is not freedom!"

"No. It sounds more like divine madness to me. Or diabolical madness, if you prefer, but the early Greeks would have called it all divine."

I rounded on Byron again. "What do you know of that man who killed himself on your front steps yesterday?"

"They are no longer my steps," Byron faintly demurred.

"*What do you know of him?*"

Byron glared at me. "Nothing. Hart would just ignore him as if he couldn't even hear his cries. I asked, but he just smiled vaguely, and changed the subject, as if he didn't know what on earth I was talking about, but was too polite to say so."

"He seemed to me a fine young man," I sullenly insisted.

"I don't doubt it," his lordship agreed, sounding smooth yet sincere.

I sighed, and at last I went over to sit by Keats. He asked, "What do you think of all this, Andrew?"

"I don't know. I just don't know. And it's hard to plan what to do, or how to take action against him, if we don't even know who or what he is. Or what he's doing, or why."

"I suppose we must just wait and see," he suggested.

"While my lady lies cold in an untimely grave, and he walks the world causing mischief."

"Even so," Keats murmured.

And we all sat there in silence for a great while.

Keats and Dionysius

Of course, as a Christian I believed in both God and the Devil, though I rarely thought about the latter and all my prayers dwelled on God's influence in the world. I had never imagined that I would directly encounter either in my life. Why would I have thought I'd even discover an angel or a demon, let alone the Devil himself? And so I didn't even know whether to take Byron seriously or not. And if we were to believe him, then I had little idea of what we might do about it. How does one fight against the Devil?

I paid a visit to the Reverend Mr Wolff, who took our Sunday service. His reaction was sceptical. "You are saying that Satan walks among us?"

"A friend of mine believes so. He is convinced that the Devil has possessed a… an acquaintance of ours."

Wolff grimaced, and then asked with an ironic smile, "Where else but in Rome?"

"Does not the Gospel of Luke say that the Devil possessed Judas and provoked his betrayal of his master?"

"*Then entered Satan into Judas Iscariot, being of the number of the twelve.*" Wolff shrugged urbanely. "Those days are long gone, Andrew."

"Are they?"

"Calling someone possessed was simply a way of understanding certain events or characteristics, certain temptations. We understand these things very differently today." Another grimace. "And do not suggest to me the Papist notion of exorcism."

I frowned. "Jesus himself performed exorcisms!"

"Again, a metaphor that does not apply to our modern times. Andrew, I suggest you read the Gospel of John. You will find no exorcisms there. John is the most useful guide to our behaviour today."

So, there was no help to be found from the Reverend. My expression must have been one of great dissatisfaction.

"Andrew, Christ died on the cross in order to defeat Satan and his ilk. Put your faith in his sacrifice."

"Yes, of course," I muttered with bowed head.

Wolff considered me for a long moment. And then he asked, "Who is this person, this acquaintance of yours? Of what do you accuse him?"

"Never mind," I replied. "It is probably nothing."

When I finally returned to our lodgings that evening, I was dismayed to find Keats lying sprawled on the sofa, and Severn standing over him with disapproval pursing his mouth and the jug of water in his hands. "He's been drinking again," Severn announced when he saw my raised brow.

"One glass," Keats protested.

"Oh yes, absolutely, one glass," Severn scoffed.

"One glass to be sociable."

I was staring at Keats. "You haven't been drinking with Hart again?"

"Of course not," he airily replied. "He is thy enemy."

Severn wasn't about to let him get away with any of this. "Lies are ugly, John. As you well know. Or you used to, at least."

Keats opened his mouth to retort, but then apparently had a change of heart. He smiled wryly at Severn, and murmured, "*Beauty is truth, and truth beauty*. Is that what you wish me to remember?"

"Yes, John."

Keats drank down some water, and then let Severn refill the glass. "If you want the truth," he said, rather subdued, "that man does serve the *finest* claret."

"Where were you?" I asked with some trepidation. "You didn't go to the palazzo, did you?"

"No. Just the trattoria." Keats waved a hand vaguely in the direction of the trattoria opposite us on the Piazza di Spagna. "And figs!" he added. "A platter of magnificent fresh figs…"

"In *January*?" That was ridiculous.

"John, please. That's too fanciful to be the truth."

Keats struggled to prop himself up on an elbow, and lay there pondering sombrely. "Unseasonable figs. What does that make me think of, Joseph?"

Severn sighed. "I'm sure I don't know. Here, drink some more water."

He did so, but then it dawned on him. "Of course! Marlowe's Faust sending Mephistopheles off for unseasonable ripe grapes for the pregnant duchess."

I frowned. "Mephistopheles, as in the character to which Byron used to compare Hart?"

"The same. Except… I called him Dionysius instead, and figs belong to Dionysius. Ivy and grapevines and figs."

This drew no more than a shrug from me. "Why is any of this significant?"

Keats looked at me. There was something sharp in his eyes, but he was still pondering as well. "Byron thinks Iago is actually the Devil incarnate. So, maybe it's not a metaphor any more. Maybe Iago is actually Dionysius."

"You can't believe that!" I protested. Severn was looking pale.

"Well," said Keats. "Maybe I half believe it."

And nothing I could say would shift him, either towards confirming the notion or denying it.

Severn had had a restless night, so I was careful not to wake him in the morning. I put the kettle on to boil, and then looked into the bedroom to see whether Keats was awake. I found that he was not only awake, but out of bed, and sitting by the windows wrapped in a blanket, looking thoughtfully down at his hands which lay, one upon the other, in his lap. He was cradling the white cornelian in a palm. One of the windows was open, so that the constant burble of the piazza's fountain was present in the room.

I murmured, "How are you this morning, John?"

He looked up at me, and smiled a little. He seemed very pale and weak, but also peaceful. "I am well, thank you, and will be fit again soon enough."

"Good. I'm making tea."

"Excellent," he responded, with his smile broadening.

We sat there together silently for a while, sipping at our first cups while they were still too hot. Once I'd poured a second cup each, Keats said, "I'm feeling very clear-headed this morning. Surprisingly so."

"I'm glad to hear it."

"You may have noticed that I hit rather a low point yesterday."

I just nodded, not so much in agreement as acceptance of this confession.

"You have been wise, my friend, and counselled me to hope. Instead I have fallen lower and lower into despair." He took a breath, and drank his tea. Then he said, "This morning it seems clear to me that I can either continue down that path, or I can choose a different one. I don't know why I couldn't make that decision myself long before now, but there it is."

"And which path have you chosen?" I asked, though I knew the answer. He deserved to tell me himself, rather than have me tell him.

"The latter," he responded with a smile. He considered me for a long moment, and then said, "Andrew, would you give me Miss Brawne's letter?"

"Of course." I slipped it out of my breast pocket, and handed it over. Then I got up, intending to let him read it in peace.

"You don't have to go."

So, I stayed, and poured more tea. And Keats read the letter slowly and carefully, once through and then twice. And he wept. But in the end he looked more profoundly content than I had ever seen him before.

Severn went out late that morning, muttering something vague about having errands to run. He hadn't returned by mid-afternoon, so Keats and I went for our regular walk without him. Determined now to work on improving his health, Keats insisted on a long wander through the parklands of the Pincian Hill.

As we walked back along the Corso, we paid little attention to the Palazzo Amara and its imposing, unchanging façade. We were, however, surprised to find a familiar figure sitting slumped at a table outside a trattoria not far from the palazzo. It was Severn, instantly recognisable despite his head hanging so low that his long brown curls hid his face.

We stood by his table for a moment, waiting for him to notice us. Eventually Keats said, "Joseph? May we join you?"

Finally he looked up and nodded, but he didn't shift up from his slump or acknowledge us in any other way. We ordered birra and a platter of antipasto.

Keats began questioning me about the position of ship's surgeon in the navy or in the East India Company: what the duties were, what qualifications were required, how easy it would be to find a place, how long the voyages would last, and so on. "You intend to seek such work, then?" I concluded, remembering that Keats already had medical training.

"Yes, I –" He looked at Severn, but he was still paying us little attention. "There is an inexorable logic to it, Andrew," Keats said, shifting forward in his chair. "If I have found the courage to hope again, then I must regain my health. Once I am healthy, I must return to England. When I am in

England, I must be with Miss Brawne. To be with her, I must marry her, and no doubt there will be children. Therefore we must have something upon which to live in a degree of comfort. But I cannot earn enough from poetry; I have tried. And so I will return to my other vocation of medicine. There you have my conclusion."

By this time even Severn was staring at him. "But, John," he faintly protested, "that was such an important decision for you, to turn away from medicine and devote your time on earth to poetry instead. It took courage, and we all admired you for it."

Keats smiled a little. "Yes, but it does not necessarily follow that in returning to medicine I must also turn away from poetry."

"With responsibilities such as work and marriage and fatherhood draining you, what can you possibly have left for poetry?"

"I am a poet, Joseph. I know that now in every cell of my body, in every charge of my life's energy. Miss Brawne understands as much, and she loves me for it. I cannot stop being what I am."

Severn had sat up by now, and had a stubborn set to his narrow jaw. "I beg your pardon, John, but that is exactly what will happen. When you gave up your studies, you said you needed to concentrate solely on poetry. If you are a poet, then how can you invite such demands and distractions into your life?"

"Because the poetry has taken root and is now a part of me. I don't need to make it my priority any more, and force all else aside, because it is simply *there*."

Severn would not be persuaded. He was about to argue further, when he glanced at me and then closed his mouth again. I stirred in my seat, ready to make my excuses and leave so that they could converse in confidence, even though of course I was deeply interested in hearing more about my friend's plans.

But Keats reached a hand to my arm to stay me. "Joseph, you can be as candid as you like in Andrew's presence. You are both my dear friends."

"Well, then." Severn briefly glowered at me from within the fall of his long hair. "I say nothing against Miss Brawne herself –"

"I thank you," muttered Keats with some sarcasm.

"– but your devotion to her forced all else aside for a time. Why should that not happen again? Would it not be best to remain independent? For the sake of your art?"

Keats sat back, and gazed up at the sky for a while, thinking on this. Or perhaps thinking on how to reply. Eventually he said, "In my insecurities about poetry, I committed my all to it for a time. In my insecurities about being loved, I held too fast to the young woman I cared about most. But those days are past, my friend, and I am secure. I can take a step back, and my life can encompass more."

"I remember how it was, John," Severn muttered darkly. "She drove you mad with her flirtations."

If anyone had dared speak to me like that of Lady Elena, I would have wanted to throw down the gauntlet. However, Keats smiled – a little coolly, it's true – and said, "That is to be forgot. I love Fanny for her brightness and her vivacity, and I was wrong to misinterpret it so. But anyway," he added, "we are a long way from where I started. What would you say, Joseph, if I became a ship's surgeon? Would you not envy me such adventures?"

Severn would not be cheered out of his disapproval. "You gave away medicine, John, and you were right to do so."

"But I kept all my medical texts. I never turned away from healing; I only concentrated on pursuing it in a different form. I have three loves," Keats declared, "and I am so full of hope today, that I am determined to possess them all."

A firm shake of the head from Severn indicated that he would argue no further. When Keats looked to me, I smiled with gentle pride. "I am deeply glad to be your friend, John."

"And I yours, Andrew."

Despair

It had been well over a month since Byron and the Shelleys had visited Cardinal Guido Rinaldi. My intention at the time had been to accompany them on another visit soon thereafter, but at first this had been postponed until after Christmas, and then I let it slip my mind. It was late January when I belatedly realised that I hadn't seen the cardinal at all for some while, with Hart or at the Vatican Library or anywhere else.

I asked the Shelleys if they would visit the cardinal again, and allow me to accompany them. Of course they kindly agreed, and we went that Friday afternoon.

We weren't, however, shown further than the front hall of the cardinal's villa. After some back-and-forthing in Italian between Shelley and the housekeeper, Shelley turned to me with a frown and announced, "The cardinal has been fasting. Apparently he has become quite ill."

Mary was pale and concerned. The housekeeper was unhappy to the point of misery. Something awful occurred to me. I said to Shelley, "Ask her if he's fasting – or if he's been starving himself."

Shelley demurred. "That's hardly an appropriate question, and even if it was, it's unlikely we'd receive an honest answer."

I turned to Mary. "Ask her! Can you make the distinction in Italian? Ask her if he's deliberately destroying himself."

Mary spoke gently with the woman for a long moment. The housekeeper didn't reply, but her mouth turned down in anticipated grief.

I clenched my fists, pushed back out onto the street, and strode away before I could intrude any further. It seemed clear to me that Adrian Hart was claiming yet another victim.

'*I am not what I am…*'

I felt restless and dissatisfied that Saturday, so I went for a walk to the south-east, past the enormous looming ruins of the Colosseum, and then I climbed the Palatine Hill. I stopped for a while on the terrace there, looking back across the Forum and its maze of arches and columns and jagged walls, much of it losing ground to trees and undergrowth. No one else was around, which perhaps intensified my feeling that the presence of centuries weighed heavily there.

I had intended walking on to the Pyramid of Cestius, and paying my respects again to little William Shelley. However, when I turned away from the view, I saw Adrian Hart loitering there in the shadows at the back of the terrace.

He stepped forward when he saw that I'd noticed him, and we slowly approached each other. He was dressed superbly and pristinely, as usual, in a royal blue coat and sage green trousers, with a pair of dark blue leather gloves held in one hand; if I didn't know better, he would seem the quintessential gentleman. As I came to a halt with about a yard between us – closer than I'd ever been to him before – I realised how very beautiful he was. I would choose Elena's happy candour over his thoughtful reserve on any day, but the brother was in his own way as compellingly attractive as his sister.

"Lieutenant Sullivan," Hart eventually murmured. "Perhaps, under the circumstances, we can dispense with the formalities of introductions."

"What circumstances are those?" I asked, bluntly on the offensive.

"Why, you being such a very good friend to my sister and her husband," he replied with an urbane smile.

Without volition, my hand rose to press against the locket at my chest. "You are not fit to speak of her."

He bowed his head in respectful acknowledgement. "And they say that chivalry is dead. I am glad that Elena has such a proper champion."

"And you dare to speak her name," I muttered. I turned aside for a moment's consideration, wondering how far I could usefully go, what I could permissibly say. Until now I had been cautious, and worked within society's expectations. I had treated Hart like the gentleman he pretended to be. But nothing about this situation was reasonable, and I was too tired to avoid the truth any longer. My head ached with the tension of everything that had been left unsaid.

When I faced him again, I found Hart was watching me with some interest. I quietly demanded, "Tell me who and what you are. I can't believe a woman like that – everything that was fair and true – was actually your sister."

"Oh, but she was," he replied with the lightest insinuation.

I ignored his tone as best I could. "A friend of mine thinks you are the Devil incarnate. Quite literally. Is that so?"

Hart laughed at this, as if it were the finest joke. "I can guess who. And is he not the one with the cloven foot?"

"Tell me what you are."

And I knew what he would reply even as I asked the question. It was as if he knew that the line had haunted me ever since I first heard it from Keats. Hart considered me for a long moment, and then intoned Iago's words: *"I am not what I am."*

I stared at him for a long while, as if I could drill out his meaning with only my gaze and the pain behind it. It occurred to me that the words could have applied to any of us at one time or another. Keats hadn't been his best, true self until only two days previous; he had not been what he was capable of being. I hadn't been, either; I had let myself be unmanned, lulled into inaction. But surely such an interpretation of the words did not apply to Hart. Surely he was taunting me with the notion that he wasn't Elena's brother, that perhaps he wasn't even a man.

Eventually I declared, "I'm not interested in guessing your riddles."

"Then what *are* you interested in, Lieutenant?"

I glanced at the gloves he carried; my own pair was back at the lodgings, and of no use to me now. Instead I declared, "You have done me great wrong, and I demand satisfaction."

Hart found this inordinately amusing. "A *duel?* How delightful!"

"You will not think it so."

"No, for I would win, and you would be dead, and where would be the fun in that?"

"Everyone who has anything to do with you ends up lost, so what's one more death to you?"

"Ah, but you are Elena's truest knight, and I have need of you yet."

It was a stirring notion, I could not deny that. However, I managed to protest. "The role of my lady's champion belongs to her husband, and he remains true to her."

"Where is Mitchell, then?" Hart spread one hand, but didn't bother making a show of looking around. "Where is he now? Why is it that *you* are here and he is not?"

"I act only on his behalf."

"And not on your own behalf? I don't believe that for a moment."

"If Captain Mitchell," I said thickly, "knows that I have reason to assist him beyond the call of duty and loyalty, that is neither here nor there."

"Come now," Hart scoffed. "He knew you had better reason to pursue me than he did."

I shook my head, struggling to understand. The only thing I could really comprehend was that Hart was lying. And yet what he said felt as profound as the truth. "No."

"*You're* the one who loved her, Sullivan. Aren't you? You're the one who really saw what she was, and loved her for herself alone."

"No."

"You cannot deny it!"

"I don't deny that I loved her –"

"Hah!" he cried, as if he'd scored a point.

"– but you cannot say that Captain Mitchell didn't. That he doesn't still. She was his *wife*."

"*You're* the one who's here," he repeated. "You're her one true knight."

"No." But I felt as if I were losing the battle. In a last effort, I forced the words out past a parched throat, a tongue that felt dry and swollen. "Captain Sir William Mitchell and Lady Elena are – were – the best people in the world. Their merit is far above my own. They were kind enough to be my friends, and I act accordingly. I would never dishonour either of them."

"Oh, *Andrew*," he said almost fondly. "Why won't you admit the truth?"

"You know nothing of the truth." The strangest thing was happening. My head ached thickly, throbbing now, as if I had received some mortal injury. I could not keep my balance, and I fell to one knee.

Hart leant close over me, and asked with great irony, "Did you not suggest that I am Lucifer, the bringer of light? Do I not illuminate all your secrets?"

"Get thee gone," I muttered. I collapsed to the ground.

Silence. Absence.

Darkness.

A friendly soul saw me back to the Piazza di Spagna that evening, flagging down a passing carriage to do so. He told me in the simplest English that I had been found lying there alone in the dark on the terrace, that he thought I must be ill. I thanked him, and left him there in the piazza, made my way upstairs, ignored the concern of my friends. After swallowing a jug of water which did little to ease me, I lay down on my bedroll, wrapped myself close in a blanket, and I put the world aside for a time.

I had a dream that night, the most vivid and compelling of dreams. I had died and gone to heaven. And Elena waited for me there, as a bride waits for her groom.

When I woke up cold and alone on my narrow bedroll in the grey light of dawn, I found that I wanted nothing further from this life. All I wanted was to die.

Disease

I was not inclined to go to church that morning. When Severn heard this, he directed a sullen glance towards me, and then headed off alone. After a while I propped myself up against the wall under the window, and sat there feeling indifferent.

Keats settled on the sofa with a book, but we didn't speak even though he was concerned enough about me to glance up at least once or twice a page. Eventually he asked, "Should I fetch Dr Clark?"

I shook my head. *No.*

"You don't seem well, Andrew."

My throat was thick and my voice rusty. Nevertheless I managed to say, "I'm fine."

When Keats seemed about to protest, I proved myself by drinking the cup of tea Severn had made, despite the fact it had gone stone cold. Keats got up and made me a fresh cup. "What happened last night?" he asked as he insisted on handing it over.

I just shook my head again. *Nothing.*

"At first I thought you'd been drinking, but that's not it, is it?"

"Leave me be, John," I whispered hoarsely. "Please."

After a moment's consideration, he nodded. Once Severn returned, the three of us spent a quiet dull Sunday together.

I didn't sleep well that night. Keats came out of the bedroom on the Monday morning, to find me sitting in the same place as yesterday, on the floor against the wall under the window. "Andrew," he murmured, sounding worried.

When he came closer, he seemed surprised to find that I was holding Captain Mitchell's locket in my hand, cradling the precious gold oval in one palm just as he'd held the white cornelian from Miss Brawne. When he glanced at me sharply, I closed my hand around it.

"Andrew, what's troubling you?" he asked quietly, not wanting to disturb Severn.

I shook my head. *I can't say.*

Keats' mouth narrowed, and he suddenly appeared determined. He turned away to boil the kettle for tea.

Everyone came to our lodgings that afternoon; Keats had organised it. I'd barely moved all day, except to hang the locket safely around my neck. I didn't place it back in its protective pouch; instead I wore the locket itself, the gold warm against my skin.

The others looked at me with varying degrees of curiosity. Mary asked, "Are you well, Andrew?"

I replied, "Yes, thank you." Which I'm sure didn't fool anyone, but no one was rude enough to challenge me on it.

Once the other six were settled around the sitting room with food and drink to hand, Keats called the gathering to order. "I am sure none of us will rest easily," he began, "unless we take some kind of decisive action against this man who calls himself Iago. We none of us have reason to think well of him, but beyond that we owe it to our friend Andrew."

Byron was sitting back in the most comfortable chair, one leg crossed over the other. He seemed a little exasperated, in a lordly kind of way. "Let's be realistic. What *can* we do? Whether you believe me or not, he's the Devil. We mere mortals can't fight him."

"You probably know him better than any of us," Keats insisted. "Are you honestly saying you never saw in him a weakness or a vulnerability?"

"*He's the Devil.* The most we can do is resist him. What can we do but get out of his way?"

"My lord," said Keats, "I trust you are not thinking of leaving Rome. We need you here."

I noticed that Fletcher glanced at Byron with some misgivings, but Byron lightly responded, "I am settled here for now."

"I think Lord Byron is correct," Severn said, though in a weak tone. "If we resist him, if we can avoid him…"

Keats seemed irritated. "Resist *what*, exactly?"

"His claret, for a start," Severn retorted.

For a moment it seemed that everyone held their breath. But then Byron urbanely supplied, "His temptations, his coercions."

"Look," said Shelley, throwing his hands in the air. "This is *not* the Devil we're dealing with. He's not even Iago. He's a man. He's just a man named Adrian Hart."

"So what do you suggest we do?" asked Keats.

"Find some way of destroying his plans. If we can work out what he's doing. Expose him so that he can't continue in society as a gentleman. Not that I –" Shelley looked around at us all, a bit defiant. "Society is overrated. But Hart relies on his acceptance as a gentleman to protect him. Let's see what he can achieve without it."

Keats grimaced. "If he had committed a crime –" At my hard glance, he amended, "If he had committed the sort of crime that the authorities would be interested in, or if we had incontrovertible evidence –"

"He *is* just a man," said Fletcher. "But surely we can do more than damage his reputation. If the British authorities won't take any action on these papers he stole, and if there's no reason for the Italian authorities to take an interest, then we are on our own. We can fight him ourselves."

"But *how*?" Keats asked. "Fight him in what way?"

"If you gents won't get your hands dirty –"

"What do you suggest? Some kind of brawl?" Keats shook his head. "It's not that I haven't punched a man to stop his cruelty, but I don't know what that would achieve in this situation. And we would be seen as the aggressors."

I shifted a little, and said, "I spoke with Hart two days ago."

They all turned to look at me in some amazement. Keats murmured, "Andrew… Why didn't you tell us?"

I had to clear my throat to continue. "I challenged him to a duel," I said to Fletcher. "He did not accept. He would not be provoked."

"Then fight him in some other way," Fletcher responded, obdurate. "If he ain't a gentleman, then don't treat him as one."

A silence stretched. Eventually Mary asked, "John, do you think him a man or the Devil?"

Keats shrugged reluctantly. "I don't know. Part of me thinks he's Dionysius. The rest of me thinks that's foolishness."

"Yes," Mary agreed in her clear voice. "He's probably just a man, but it's hard to shake the feeling that there's something more to it."

"Either way, I'm not sure what to do for the best." He glanced at me again. "We have to do something, though."

"Perhaps we can't do anything about Hart," Mary suggested. "Perhaps we can only do something about the people he's hurting." And she looked directly at me. I am ashamed to say that I cringed; I couldn't bear her sympathy for my own turmoil. But she only said, "Andrew, we should visit Cardinal Rinaldi again. And this time, we should insist on seeing him, talking with him."

I didn't want to move from where I sat. But she was right. And she wasn't going to let me deny it. "Yes," I said eventually. "Yes, all right, we should."

Mary was coming to collect me at two the following afternoon. Keats politely yet firmly made me get up, and wash myself, and put on fresh clothes. He looked pensive when he saw that I was still wearing my captain's locket, but he didn't ask for my thoughts and I didn't volunteer them.

When Mary and I reached the cardinal's villa, it was apparent that the housekeeper recognised us. Mary talked to her, gently but persistently insisting that we be allowed to see the cardinal. "Apparently all he'll take is a little water," Mary told me. And it seemed the housekeeper was in such despair that she would try anything, because soon we were shown into the cardinal's bedroom.

The place was opulent, all marble and red silks with gold tassels. In the midst of the finery lay the cardinal. I might not have recognised him, he seemed so reduced. Pale and too thin, and parched, and his worldly confidence wrecked.

Mary sat on a chair by the bed, and spoke to him softly in Italian. I hovered by the foot of the bed, half hidden by the curtains and one of the posts. The cardinal glanced at me every now and then, however, as if he knew we had something in common.

Eventually Mary asked, "What would you like to say to the cardinal, Andrew?"

I walked closer to her, and the cardinal and I regarded each other carefully. He seemed as hopeless as I felt. "Tell him I understand," I asked Mary. When the cardinal nodded in weary response, I said, "Tell him I talked with Adrian Hart three days ago."

A brief exchange in quiet Italian. "Go on," said Mary.

"And ever since, I have wanted nothing more than to die."

She stared up at me with the greatest sorrow. "Andrew…"

"Tell him!" I waited, and then I added, "Tell him I know it's wrong, and *he* knows it's wrong, but I want to die."

The cardinal reached a weak hand towards me. I sat down on the edge of the bed, and grasped it in my own. My eyes prickled – but I had not wept for Elena, and I would not weep for myself or for this man. The cardinal murmured something, which Mary translated: "You are a good man, and you mustn't die."

I sighed. "It's going to be a struggle," I said directly to him, "but let's make a deal: I won't if you won't."

And when Mary had conveyed that, he nodded, and he clasped my hand with what little strength he had left. We settled in for the afternoon, and after a while, the cardinal allowed Mary to spoon-feed him from a small bowl of soup.

Friends – February 1821

Having no better ideas, I again took to sitting on the garden wall at the Palazzo Amara each evening, watching Hart as he quietly went about his business. Mostly he read books and newspapers, or wrote letters. I sat there idly pondering Byron's notions – but if Hart were the Devil, he was a remarkably inactive one. There was certainly no flying off to fetch unseasonable grapes or indeed figs. The most I ever caught him at was smiling with an irritatingly charming wickedness as he wrote.

On the first Saturday of February, Hart had a visitor: I was dismayed to see Lord Byron being shown into the room where he and Hart had sat together so often before. Byron seemed rather nervous to me, though this only manifested itself in a slight uncertainty. Hart stood to greet him, and they exchanged polite words while Byron hovered not far from the door.

After a while, Hart took a step backwards into the room. And Byron took a step towards him. They continued talking together, in longer sentences and with slightly more relaxed postures. Hart took another step back, and again Byron followed him as if drawn to him. This time Byron took two steps to Hart's one. I cursed under my breath. What the hell did Byron think he was *doing* coming here? And anyway, how did one man manage to seduce another by walking away from him?

I stirred restlessly on the wall, giving serious thought to jumping down and interrupting them, no matter what the consequences. It wasn't as if Hart didn't know I was there. But that was when I thought I glimpsed a faint light moving behind one of the otherwise darkened windows of the palazzo's library. As I looked directly, it vanished, but after a long moment – in which Byron took three steps forwards to Hart's one step back – the light moved past the second of the full-length glass doors. And I belatedly realised what was happening.

I climbed into the nearest tree and clambered down to the ground, then made my way as carefully as possible to the furthest door of the library. Tapped quietly at the glass. The light was immediately shielded, but I soon saw Fletcher making his way over, peering through the darkness to identify me. He lifted his chin as if to ironically observe, *What a surprise to see you here.* Then he let me in.

"What are you *doing* here?" I whispered, although I'd already surmised the answer.

"Having another go at finding those papers for you, and Mr Shelley's letters."

"And Byron…?"

Fletcher gave me a sardonic look. "Creating a distraction."

I snorted at this. "Of course, Hart *knows* you're here."

"Then he probably knows you're here, too," Fletcher observed. "Doesn't he?"

"Yes," I admitted.

Fletcher shrugged, and opened his lantern again. "Then why waste the chance for another sneak around?"

Well, he had a point. Not having a light, I started examining the piles of papers nearest the doors, where there was just enough moonlight to make out the gist of any lettering of a reasonable size.

Naturally we achieved nothing at all, for Hart did not intend that we should. The effort made me feel a little more enlivened, however, and Fletcher seemed glad of it, too.

Eventually a slamming door and hurried footsteps made us lift our heads. Fletcher nodded farewell to me, shielded his lantern, and hastened back into the palazzo itself. I waited a few discreet moments, headed back into the garden, and made my escape.

Despite everything, it seemed that I had friends. Even if we were all lost, my friends were with me. It didn't occur to me at the time that could be the worst aspect of all.

I didn't attend church on the following Sunday either. I wasn't entirely sure whether this was because I had lost faith in God or in the Reverend Mr Wolff, or if I felt tainted by association with Hart. In any case, Severn didn't approve of me missing the service, nor of my general lethargy. He was hardly even talking to me at the moment beyond the necessary exchanges involved in sharing lodgings and a good friend. Otherwise Severn just considered me with thin lips, and then turned away. Perhaps even Keats didn't notice, however, as I continued to be rather withdrawn myself.

Confronting Hart had shaken me at some deep level. Perhaps even – well, if he had not destroyed my foundations then he'd realigned them, and I must take the time to adjust. Not to align myself with Hart so much as to take him into account. Day after day I either trailed around after Hart or just sat there in our sitting room, trying to work this out. He was evil, he was truly evil, and must be fitted into my world as such.

Severn remained withdrawn and disapproving and shaken, too – which, other than the disapproval, was much as he'd been before I'd recovered his sketch of Alcibiades from the Palazzo Amara. This made me wonder how much in common Severn and I had. Whether Severn had recently confronted Hart as well, or been forced to take him into account. Whether Severn also felt compromised.

But I didn't think about Hart all the time. At night I lay sleepless, restless on my bedroll, and I dreamed of my lady, my angel Elena, and of how she awaited me in heaven.

Keats insisted on taking me to dine with the Shelleys. Severn had been invited, too, but he had withdrawn so far into himself that his excuses were accepted; I wasn't entirely sure why mine were not, for I was sure Keats was aware what poor company I had become.

When we got to the Shelleys' hotel, we found our hosts welcoming and polite, but Mary's shoulders were rigid and her mouth was set in a frosty line, while Shelley was evasive, clumsy, hapless. For a while we pretended all was well, but once we'd each had a glass of wine Keats asked the question that was required of people who are friends rather than acquaintances: "Is something amiss? Is there anything we can do?"

Shelley demurred. "No, everything is fine."

"Perhaps this has proved to be a bad day for entertaining guests."

Mary sighed, glanced at her husband and then looked at me directly. "We have been discussing whether to return to Pisa."

"Oh," was my only reply to this unwanted news.

"I am the one who proposed we return," Shelley admitted. "Mary has been arguing that we should stay."

"Thank you," I said to her.

Keats added, "I'm sure we all hope you both decide that you'll stay."

But this only aggravated Shelley. "Mary's curiosity is piqued, there's nothing more to it than that."

For the first time, I saw Mary's cheeks flush. "I am also concerned for our friends."

"You were never one to leave well enough alone!"

She retorted, "You used to like that about me."

Shelley made a show of explaining the matter to us, when really he was talking at his wife. "Mary simply wants to know who or what your Iago is, no matter what the consequences. I don't think she'd care if she was dragged down to Hell for eternity, as long as that meant she knew for certain that he was the Devil."

Mary sighed in frustration. "You are exaggerating."

"Am I, indeed?" he retorted.

"Yes, especially as you believe he's no more nor less than a man. And if he were, if you really believed that, then where's the harm in staying?"

To which Shelley had no answer. The argument subsided, and eventually the awkwardness was shaken off, and by the end of the meal all was pleasant again.

'Death's the end of all...'

"She is not yours," said Keats.

I was sitting in my customary place, on the floor against the wall under the window. Cradling Captain Mitchell's locket in my hand, and occasionally dwelling on the miniature of my lady Elena.

"She is not yours to dream of."

I rolled my head against the wall the better to cast him a sullen glare.

"Andrew, you are forgetting your better self. Your generosity and your courage."

"What is that to you?"

"You are my friend."

"She is my love."

"Lady Elena may have been many things, Andrew, but she cannot be that."

It was outrageous, really, that he should say so. "You owe me more, John. I have done nothing but encourage you in *your* love."

"Ah," said Keats quite gently, "but Miss Brawne has committed herself to me, with her mother's blessing. We are engaged to be married. You cannot say the same."

"Elena is free now," I insisted.

"She was another man's wife while alive."

"But she is free now." And I whispered, "My angel Elena."

Keats' patience turned to exasperation. "Andrew – even if there were a heaven, you know very well it would not work like that. She would still be the wife of Captain Mitchell. Your friend. Your superior officer."

"Leave me be!"

"You owe him more than this. You owe her memory more than this. You owe yourself far more than this!"

I clutched the locket hard against my chest, turned my face to the wall like a recalcitrant child, and I ignored him.

Keats insisted on me joining him on an expedition one day. A carriage bore us south along the Appian Way, until we reached a small jumbled ruin in a field. Keats hired torches from a man who sat slumped amidst the stones, and we descended into the earth itself.

An ancient treacherous staircase led down into darkness, some of the marble still in place, but the rest broken away to reveal the living stone and compacted dirt. We made it down safely to an open space, visible only within the light from our torches.

The catacombs, burial place of the early Christians. Keats paused a moment as if getting his bearings, and then led me down a corridor. The walls were lined with cavities, some enclosed by carved tablets or tiles, and some open. Tombs had been dug into the floor. A few freestanding stone coffins lined the walls. Thankfully the air was dry, though it was not pleasant.

There were bones everywhere, along with shreds of shrouds, dust and cobwebs. Centuries old. Some of the bodies lying in the niches were whole, but otherwise bones were strewn across the floors of the galleries and crypts, or swept into corners like piles of autumn leaves.

We wandered for what seemed an hour or so, both anxiously trying to keep our bearings. And then at last Keats paused. Looked around him for a moment, and then fixed me with a contemplative stare. "This is all there is, Andrew."

"You do not believe –" I faltered.

"I *know*. This is all there is. If you die, you will not find yourself in heaven with your lady. You will not be anywhere. Your soul will be extinguished, like this torch will be. Soon your body will be nothing but bones. Eventually dust. You will not know it. You will not be happy or loved. *This* is all there is."

It was the bleakest of prospects. And it was probably true.

We were silent. The carriage bore us to a place that had already become familiar. The Pyramid of Cestius, with the scatter of graves at its feet. Keats and I wandered for a while in the wholesome air and fitful sunshine. The grass was long, and there were a few early daisies and violets. "I love violets," Keats murmured, contemplating the tiny dark purple blooms at his feet. Sheep grazed contentedly. Little William Shelley lay slumbering in his last bed.

"There is peace," I said after a while. "It is not just bones and darkness. There is peace."

"There is peace," Keats agreed.

We dismissed the carriage, and spent the afternoon rediscovering a sense of tranquillity.

Hope

"Adrian Hart," I at last concluded, "makes us forget our better selves. Within his orbit we become our worse selves."

"*Yes*, my friend," Keats responded, his eyes fierce. "He lets us snare ourselves in our own untruths."

"No matter who or what he is, we must stir ourselves, and take action against him."

"It is as if we have been dwelling on disease for too long, forgetting that we have the power to heal ourselves."

I reflected, "He is the most subtle of devils, if devil he is."

"We have let ourselves feel tainted. Tarnished."

My dear friend Keats and I were in his bedroom at our lodgings, Keats with his rear propped on the foot of the bed, and I leaning by the window. The fountain burbled on below us with newfound purpose.

"But what can we do? If we are to remain gentlemen, how can we act against him, when he does nothing? When he lets us condemn ourselves?"

Keats came to join me at the window. There was a determined set to his jaw that I had not seen before. "There is one thing we can do. He has no entitlement to any of the papers he has piled in his library, he has no rights to those items. He is clearly in the wrong there."

"Yes," I agreed.

"If it were not an impossible task, I would see them returned to their owners."

I nodded. "As would I. Though we cannot. So what can we do instead?"

Everyone gathered together in our living room. Keats and I reprised our conversation.

It was Severn, this time, who pointed out the impracticalities. "Those hundreds of thousands of papers! How could we even determine who they belong to, let alone return them all? Shelley's name would be on his letters, but mine wasn't on my sketch. And even with the letters, would you return them to the writer or the recipient? And there are too many! It would take *years*."

"It is impossible," Keats agreed.

"Then what do you propose?"

"That we destroy them all, and make sure he has no further use of them. No further harm could be done."

The others considered this with thoughtful frowns.

Fletcher said, "For what my opinion's worth, I think we should do it. We are men of action, Mr Sullivan, and it's time we remembered that."

"How do we destroy them, then?" asked Mary.

"Fire," said Keats.

"But the library!" she protested. "The books…"

Severn added, "We won't have a chance to move all the papers out into the garden."

"That can't be helped," said Byron. Which surprised me from a man who carried his library around Europe with him in several chests. But then, I supposed that a lord would consider anything to be easily replaced. "Who knows what he's secreted amongst the books? The whole lot must go."

"I take your point, my lord," Mary said, "but it grieves me. Even if we could each rescue a volume or two… Something might be saved."

Keats argued, "We have no more right to the books or the papers than Iago does."

"Then we have no right to destroy them," she retorted.

"We have to do something about the papers," I said. "Or, I do. No one has to be part of this if they don't want to. You've already done more for me and for Captain Mitchell than I could ever have expected."

"You have been the most excellent of friends, Andrew," Keats said.

Shelley spoke for the first time. "I, for one, am a part of this. My letters are in that library. Well, I hope that they are, for we have no way of finding them otherwise."

"I have a question for you," I said to him. "For all of us, but for you in particular, Shelley." I took a moment to gather my thoughts, so that I could say it as succinctly as possible. "I have been used to thinking of each of these papers as representing a soul. Some of you will consider that foolish at best. But if we destroy them with fire as John suggests, then it will be as if they are burning in Hell. Can that be wise?"

"No," said Shelley, "it won't be like that. It will be a clean start. It will be a purification."

"You wouldn't mind if your letters were burned?"

"It would be far better than knowing *he* has the use of them."

"Is that how you would feel, Joseph," I asked, "if your sketch was still there?"

"Yes."

I nodded. "Then that is what I am going to do. None of you has to join me."

Keats looked around at the others, and they each nodded, whether promptly or reluctantly. "We will join you."

The Hundredth Day

And so we began planning. I wanted to take action soon, before any of us lost our nerve. Fletcher discovered from Hart's servants that he was expected to be absent that Friday evening.

Mary asked, "How did you ask them, Fletcher? Have you not just alerted Iago of our intentions?"

"All due respect, Mrs Shelley," Fletcher responded heavily, with a meaningful glance at me and then at Severn, "he'll know one way or another. There's no helping that."

"There's a reception at the British Consulate," Byron confirmed. "He's been invited to attend, and he seems forever willing to humour them."

"All right," I concluded. "Then we'll make it Friday evening, at about ten o'clock." It would be the hundredth day since Keats, Severn and I had come to Rome. A hundred days of confusion, error and apathy would come to an end, one way or another. Friday the twenty-third of February 1821.

I felt alive again.

Seven Souls Strong

Perhaps it was an odd sight; I could hardly tell any more. The seven of us gathered on the front steps of the Palazzo Amara with unlit torches in our hands. We paused, and to be honest I had not thought about the door which would no doubt be locked and barred. Hart would know to expect us, after all. But Fletcher stepped past us, and simply turned the handle, pushed it open. I stepped through first into the dark hallway, and then the others followed, and then Fletcher came last, closing the door firmly behind us.

The house was quiet. We waited through long moments, but there wasn't any sign of occupation; I had watched Hart leave for the reception an hour before. Neither of the servants appeared, though we assumed they must be there. I had agreed with Fletcher that he should warn them for their own safety once the fire had taken hold.

Fletcher set down the covered lantern he'd brought; he and I used spills to light everyone's torches. Then, bearing flames, we walked into the library. We opened the doors that led out to the garden, so that the fire wouldn't starve for want of air.

When I turned around, I saw that Mary had selected a book to save; I found out later that it was the bound collection of her parents' essays. Byron seemed to pick a volume at random; when he examined the spine, he huffed an ironic laugh, as if amused at how apt a choice it was. He slipped it into his jacket pocket. I took the Vico.

Then we all looked at each other for a long moment. It wasn't too late to withdraw. Severn seemed nervous; Shelley was pale but determined; Byron was cool and removed. Finally Keats nodded at me once, and he took a winding path through the papers, and lowered his torch to set the furthest pile alight.

As Keats walked back towards the door, I followed his example, setting fire to a mound of papers by the windows.

"Everyone," said Fletcher gruffly. "We must all be a part of this."

Mary was the next, and then Shelley, starting fires at different places in the room, away from the door. The flames were slowly taking hold. Smoke was already starting to obscure the ceiling. Byron put his torch to a pile in the middle of the room. Fletcher nodded at Severn, telling him without words to go ahead. And then, once we were all gathered near the door again, Fletcher lowered his own torch to the nearest papers.

As these flickering flames caught hold, the hallway was suddenly aglow – and the master of the house stood silhouetted at the doorway. Adrian Hart. He seemed as calm and collected as ever, pristine and unruffled. The seven of us stared at him silently while the fire burned behind us, and tendrils of smoke began circling our shoulders.

Hart slowly took off his gloves. "Well, well," he said urbanely. "Unexpected guests. And I was not here to offer hospitality."

"You cannot say you did not expect us," I countered thickly.

A polite inclination of his head as if to acknowledge the truth of this. A polite smile, offered to all of us, with a finishing flourish in Severn's direction. For a long moment I thought Hart would manage not to notice that we had set fire to his library. But eventually he wandered past us, and stood there surveying the blaze. It was already beyond control, beyond repair. Hart did not pass comment on the situation.

None of us should have remained; it was becoming dangerous. "Mary," I said. "We are done here, and I would see you safe. I would see you all safe now."

And yet we all stayed there, as if we could not move our feet. Hart didn't move either. We were all watching him, wary. Fascinated.

He in turn seemed fascinated by the fire. "I'm impressed," he said at last. "An interesting move, Lieutenant. You have accomplished something despite yourself."

"I have remembered myself," I insisted, forcing myself to form the words. Perhaps it was the surging smoke, but my throat seemed vastly reluctant. "I have remembered my better self at last. You would have had me forget."

Hart turned, and looked at me very directly. "What would you have forgotten, Andrew?"

"Courage. Selflessness. My best qualities. I am here because of them."

"And your lady?" he prompted with a presumptuous smile turning the corner of his mouth.

"In her service. In her memory."

He nodded, considering this. But then he let me be, and he turned to the others. "What of the rest of you? None of you knew Elena. None of you even knew her champion until a few months ago."

"I am here," Keats declared very slowly, "because you bring lies and death wherever you go. And I stand for truth and healing."

Hart deigned to be amused while the flames grew higher. "And you, Mrs Shelley? You are looking delightfully fierce. What do you stand for?"

She drew herself taller. "The intellect. The enquiring mind. The examined life."

"Is there none of you, then, who will stand for the maternal instinct?"

Shelley stepped up beside his wife. "We both stand for that. For the child we have; for the children who are lost to us. For love." And he seemed almost as fierce as Mary then. "I stand for love, of which you know nothing."

"And I," said Byron, "for a man's proper pride."

Hart favoured him with a fondly intimate look. "I think I preferred you craven and begging, my lord."

Fletcher stood by his chosen master. "I stand for loyalty and faith – and I will not have you speak thus of a man who deserves nothing but respect."

The heat and the smoke were beginning to overwhelm us. And yet none of us moved.

Finally Hart turned to Severn. "And what of you, Joseph?" he asked with something of gentleness in his tone. "Do you stand against me, too?"

Severn's sidelong gaze was fixed to the floor. After a while he said rather weakly, "I stand for beauty."

Hart bowed in a gentlemanly fashion. "And I *am* beautiful, am I not? Extraordinarily so."

Severn trembled – shook for a while. Adrian Hart was beautiful, it was true. None of us could have argued with that. And yet at last Severn defied him. "The clothes, the surface, all that I have painted of you – it is perfection. And yet underneath, just below the beautiful skin –"

The ever-present smile fell away. "Severn!" roared Hart in warning, his hand clenching into a fist.

"*Joseph*," cried Keats in anguish.

"– below the seduction is vileness and corruption."

Hart was moved to fury. His beautiful face twisted into ugly rage. Was this a betrayal? It must be, for him to feel it so personally. I had never seen Hart anything but calm and contained. But now… now we saw the truth, and in this moment Adrian Hart looked nothing at all like Elena. Hart lifted his hand towards Severn, pushed it towards him with his arm outstretched, and took a step in his direction.

The smoke billowed, confusing our senses, pricking our eyes. The flames had become a furnace, reflecting off the polished floor as if we stood on the surface of a molten lake.

"You, of all these, are my creature," said Hart.

"I am *not*," replied Severn. His defiance was timid, but it was defiance nevertheless.

"*Severn!* Come with me now."

I could not imagine how Severn resisted when Hart's words pulled even at me. And yet Severn dropped to his knees and folded his hands before him. "*Our Father which art in heaven, hallowed be thy name…*"

"Joseph," murmured Keats, stepping towards him, "dearheart."

None of us could ever quite agree on what happened next. But these things were clear.

A flash from Hart's reaching hand –

Keats shielding Severn with his own body –

Keats falling, his waistcoat singed over his sturdy heart –

Severn dragging his dearest friend into his arms with a forsaken wail –

All of us standing there staring in horror –

Even Hart standing there sadly contemplating this ruination –

We gathered around our friend, Mary falling to her knees beside him to find and treat his wound –

And Hart turned away, head lowered, as if even he could not bear that Keats was hurt – Hart turned away, and he walked into the flames.

At my shout, Fletcher rushed to my side, and we tried to follow. But the fire was too vigorous now, and Hart had already vanished within it. It was impossible that he could have made it through to the doors, and yet we saw and heard no more of him. If the flames consumed him then he died without a cry, without a groan.

The others had carried Keats through to the relative coolness of the hall, and knelt or stood around him where he lay cradled by Joseph. "You should have let him take me," Severn was mumbling through his tears. "What need have I to live, if you should die?"

"Dearheart," Keats said weakly. And I knew from his voice alone that the hurt was a mortal one. "Is he gone? Did he let you go?"

"Yes," said Severn miserably. "John, my soul… my tattered useless soul."

"Your soul is strong and whole, and it is your own," came the stout reply. "It is not in my keeping, nor in Iago's."

Mary said, "Rest quietly, John. Shelley, Fletcher – you must fetch help. Find a surgeon."

"It is too late," said Keats. And he would know; he was a surgeon himself. "Stay with me, my friends."

We all assented to this, though struck with horror. I could have borne losing anyone other than Keats. I could not bear this. And for Severn's sake, too! Even in that moment, I knew that if I had that time over again, if I could have prevented Keats from protecting Severn from Hart's maliciousness, I would have done so without a second thought.

If I had never known before, despite the loss of Elena, I knew it then: death was irrevocable. This was disaster, and it could not be undone.

Keats cast a glance around at everyone, but then called me to him. "Andrew. Another mission, once this one is fulfilled."

I knelt at his side. "You have helped me to fulfil it. He is gone."

"I am glad." A tiny smile twitched at his lips, but then he gasped as the pain almost took him under. In a panic, he fumbled in his trouser pocket, then found the white cornelian, and held it in a fist against his chest. Over his heart. When he gathered himself again, John seemed to know he must be brief. "Go to my lady. Go to Miss Brawne. Tell her that my last thoughts were of her. My last words were of my love for her. My darling girl."

"I will, John. Of course I will. She shall know how brave and loving and true you are."

The weakest brush of his hand against the back of mine in gratitude. The light within him flickered and dimmed. And then he was gone. I grasped his hand too late, and lowered my head. And I wept. We all did.

Darkling We Mourn

We carried the body of John Keats out to the front steps. People were gathering in the street. Water was brought to prevent the fire spreading. Figures were hurrying past us in and out of the palazzo now; Hart's elegant form wasn't one of them, or not that I saw.

Fletcher went to find Dr James Clark. When he came, we were still all gathered around Keats, stunned and silent. Clark examined him, opened his shirt to view the wound on his chest; it was only a small wound, but oddly shaped, and with strange marks or bruising. Like nothing I'd ever seen in battle. Clark slipped a hand down to feel at his back for an exit wound. "What happened here?" he asked, confused. "What caused this?"

"A pistol?" I suggested. It had been unclear, though I remembered Hart's hand outstretched, and then something glinting.

Shelley said slowly, dazedly, "It was more like a bolt of electricity."

Clark frowned up at him.

"There was a flash," said Byron, "but I thought it a reflection of light on a knife or a sword in his hand."

"This was not caused by a sword," said Clark flatly.

Byron shrugged, and turned away.

"Lightning," said Mary. "Not electricity, but a bolt of lightning."

"I will have to examine him properly," Clark concluded. "You were within the palazzo? Did something explode in the fire? This might have been a fragment of some kind, made into shrapnel as it were."

"No doubt that's it," I said, dully supposing that we probably wouldn't want anyone enquiring too closely into what had happened.

As if overhearing this thought, Clark stared harder at me. "Was there anyone else? Is there anyone hurt?"

"No," I replied.

"The two servants are safe," said Fletcher. I was too numb to be glad, but I did feel relieved at this news.

"The man who lived here," I said very slowly. "Adrian Hart. He was there in the library. In the midst of the blaze. Beyond our reach. There'll be a body for you to examine."

Clark was still looking at me, as if he knew he wasn't being told the full story. But at last he nodded. And then he stood, and spoke to some of the nearby locals.

Eventually the six of us trailed down the street, following Clark, and Keats' body lying ungainly on a handcart. Byron had taken pity on our friend, and spread his fine coat over Keats' face and torso. People looked on as we passed, not caring beyond curiosity. I wept once more, helplessly.

There was no body found in the ruins of the library at the Palazzo Amara. There was no sign that Adrian Hart had even been there that evening. In fact, there were firm reports of him still being at the reception at the British Consulate at a time when the fire was known to have taken hold, and Dr Clark was already on the front steps examining our friend. No one knew where Hart was now, however, so there was a general air of confusion and unease.

"He couldn't have reached the doors," I insisted. "He couldn't have escaped through to the garden."

Fletcher agreed. "The fire was too fierce."

"Too fierce for a man," said Byron. "If man he was."

"You still think him the Devil incarnate?" I asked, somewhat exasperated.

"Flames would almost be his natural element," Byron observed.

"He killed our friend!" I cried. "He killed the finest man of all of us. And you are still weaving your stories and your… your –"

"My what?" his lordship asked dangerously.

"Your *nonsense*. John knew it was nonsense, you know. He knew there was nothing more beyond this life."

"He had an imagination, unlike you."

"There's no God, no Devil. No heaven nor hell."

"You should have kept to what you know, Lieutenant. Hauling in sails, and – and firing your phallic cannons, and dancing jigs!"

"Please!" Mary cried, suddenly there between us with her skirts swirling and her eyes bright and damp. "*Please*, my friends. The best of us is lost, it's true. And this petty bickering is the last thing he would have wished for us."

I inclined my head in obedience, lowered it further still in humility – and saw that Byron did the same.

"Please," Mary repeated, in softer tones. "We have arrangements to make."

This was Rome, of course, and anyone not a Catholic must be buried beyond the city walls. Not only that, but it must be done at night, as if surreptitiously. As if in shame. Clark, however, managed to gain a dispensation allowing us to bury our friend in the earliest hours of daylight, in the peace and the hope of dawn.

Early on the Monday morning, our small procession walked through the quiet streets, led by the Reverend Mr Wolff and trailing the carriage bearing what remained to us of John Keats. The last hour of the night was cold and still; the sky dark but for a slight glow to the east. None of us spoke.

We left the city behind, and then reached the graves by the ruins of the Aurelian Wall just as the sun broke across the horizon. A grave had been prepared at the edge of these restful fields. It wasn't far from where Shelley and Mary's son William lay, and beyond little Willmouse the white marble pyramid rose tall and graceful. The gravedigger stood respectful and distant under one of the trees, the pale green of new leaves bright against his dark clothes, the dark trunk.

Wolff read the service; just the simplest version possible, we had asked him. Even Severn hadn't seemed keen to make more of this than Keats himself would have wanted. And then we watched the coffin being lowered into the ground. Keats lay within it, in his finest clothes such as they were, with the cornelian and Miss Brawne's last letter in his hands. The gravedigger came forward, and steadily began filling in the grave, with dark brown earth that seemed wholesome to me. Perhaps it wasn't appropriate or expected, but we stayed.

The sun was shining fully now, warming us. Inevitably providing a sense of renewal, which both mocked and comforted.

At last there was nothing to see but a mound of raw earth amidst the long grass. Severn broke his silence to ask the gravedigger to cover the bareness with turfs of daisies. There were carved and painted daisies on the ceiling above his bed in our lodgings. "Violets," I said. "He liked violets best."

Severn stared at me a bit resentfully. But he said, "Violets as well, then." And the gravedigger agreed.

Eventually we left. Wolff had already gone, of course. The rest of us, this sorry truncated group of six disparate acquaintances, walked back into the city, which was awake now and bustling. We went our separate ways.

Severn and I returned to the lodgings which no longer felt like home. There seemed to be no reason any longer for us to share the place. We seemed like strangers to each other. Severn went through to the bedroom and lay himself down on Keats' bed. Slept, in order to escape the day and all the implications of our loss.

I sat on the sofa, and contemplated once more my captain's locket. After a while, without opening it, without looking again at Lady Elena or her brother, I carefully wrapped it in the silk and the canvas, and slipped it into the pouch, which I placed around my neck. Then I lay down, too, stretching out on the sofa. And I thought about John resting now in a place that was almost beautiful enough for him. And I murmured to myself, "There is peace."

The six of us met one last time, in Byron's hotel rooms. Fletcher was already packing his lordship's books into the six chests. The tens and hundreds of books that Keats had arranged in his shirtsleeves, while I read the translation of Vico and Byron complimented my friend.

"Still no news of Hart?" Fletcher asked me while the two of us waited for the others. He knew what my answer would be.

"Nothing. The authorities are at a loss."

Fletcher grimaced. "Nothing unexpected there, then."

The British Consulate had been hounding the Italians for a resolution on behalf of their late favourite, but were themselves embarrassed by the way Hart had disappeared so thoroughly, which did not exactly speak to his good intentions. Their cries of foul play had dwindled. It was generally assumed that Keats must have died as a result of the fire, and with his murderer gone it seemed useless to push for further action.

"They finally found Hart's landlord," I added. "The owner of the palazzo."

"Yes?" Again, he knew what I would say.

"Dead. Perhaps by his own hand. His heir is an obscure relative from somewhere near Milan; he won't be here in Rome for weeks yet, apparently."

Fletcher just lifted his chin in acknowledgement, and returned to the books.

At last Severn arrived, and Shelley and Mary, and then Byron came out of his bedroom. I passed on the little news I had already given Fletcher, and we sat there in silence, contemplating matters while Fletcher quietly worked on.

Eventually Mary asked, "Is there nothing more to be done, then? I cannot believe that…"

"I have run out of ideas," I confessed. "Until Hart appears again, whether here or elsewhere. What more can we do?"

"I don't know."

"At least we stopped him here. We ended his dealings in Rome."

"Yes." Mary sounded oddly subdued, however, and I knew she was unconvinced.

"And there were state secrets involved. The papers. There is still the need for discretion."

"He killed our dear friend!" she cried out in agony, turning the full force of her distraught gaze upon me.

Severn winced bitterly, and shrunk further into himself.

"Yes," I agreed, feeling both soft and raw. But then I challenged her: "You are returning to Pisa, are you not?"

"We are," said Shelley. "It is our home for now. There is our son to consider."

"Then you agree that there is nothing more to be done."

Mary threw her hand towards me in frustrated anger. "You tried to do more for the sake of Lady Elena. You tried to avenge *her* death."

"And look what good that did," I muttered, bowing my head. A strained moment passed. Then I confessed, "I myself am returning to Naples. I will wait there for Captain Mitchell and the *Boadicea*. It is over. For now, at least." I corrected myself: "No, it is over."

"We owe John Keats more than this," Byron muttered. "He was worth so much more than he ever received in life. In some ways it is too late now of course – but then it is never too late for the sake of his poetry. His *Hyperion* fragment; it is a fine thing that must survive him."

Shelley announced, "I am planning a poem. An elegy for Keats. I shall call it *Adonais*."

I stared at him in astonishment. "You cannot tell the story. You cannot say what has really happened." I found that I had stood, and was towering over him. Over them all. "The things I have told you, the secrets I have shared about my captain and his lady… I must ask you all to swear again that you shall not reveal them."

Eventually they all swore, most with a shrug. There was some desultory conversation. More regrets expressed that we could do so little for the man we had all admired so deeply. And then our unlikely band finally parted ways. It was over.

It was time to go home.

To Miss Frances Brawne

My dear Miss Brawne – for I have been setting out this account for your sake as well as my own. Miss Brawne, I write these last words as we await the tide at the mouth of the Thames. Soon I will visit you, and give you this volume in person. And we will talk of John Keats, the man we have both held so dear.

The months have been long since his death, and there have been many of them. The demands of the service have not allowed me to return to England before now, not for any reasonable length of time. But I do not complain, for it has given me the chance to consider the story, to contemplate the truth. To think long and hard about the hero of this tale, and the villain. I have Keats' seven volumes of Shakespeare with me, and I have been reading them through for the wisdom and insight they impart. And yet some mysteries remain.

Well, the truth was never very clear, and was soon obscured. You will have read Shelley's poem *Adonais*, which was honest in its grief and its valuation of Keats, but which was misleading or plain wrong about so much else. To think of our mutual friend imagined as wilting into death from his illness, to think of him as laid low by a bad review – when you and I know that he was a feisty, wonderful, adventurous man.

And so I decided to write down the real story, as I understood it at the time. As I try to understand it now. Even if you and I are the only ones who ever read it. I do not think I will even show this to Captain Mitchell, though perhaps I owe it to him. No, it will be only you and I. That is what must be, and you will understand that I am trusting you with my soul. My soul on paper. But John trusted you with his heart, that finest, bravest and most generous part of him, so I cannot believe I am doing wrong.

Shelley did write some fine things in his elegy, which I trust brought you some comfort. *He is a portion of the loveliness which once he made more lovely.* If you ever visit Rome, you will find that this is literally true as well as true in spirit. I often imagine him lying there in peace, under the abundant grass and the violets, with the proofs of your love in his hands. Keeping company with Willmouse, the child of sunshine and laughter.

You will have heard about poor Shelley's end, of course. Drowned with two friends, when his boat went down in a storm in the Gulf of Spezia. A book of John's poems in his jacket pocket, bent back as if he'd been reading it even as they ran into trouble. Mary Shelley has returned to England with their young son Percy Florence, who is heir to a baronetcy. She is writing, still, and for that we must all be thankful.

But now I hear that Lord Byron is fighting for the Greek cause of independence in a pestilential place named Missolonghi. The sturdy and ever loyal Fletcher is with him, of course, and yet I fear for him.

Of all people, it is Joseph Severn who is doing well. He was the only one of us to remain in Rome, and he was feted there as a friend of Keats, as a painter of portraits, as a steady man of character. Shelley of course had lauded his care of John in *Adonais*, and it seems that no one knows any different any more. I hear that he is to marry well. It is unexpected, but not undeserved. And I must remember – John Keats died for his sake. That must mean something, after all. The sacrifice has not been wasted.

Severn told me once – he was very careful to quote our friend exactly. He told me that Keats once wrote to a friend: *A man should have the fine point of his soul taken off to become fit for this world.*

It is a fascinatingly ambiguous statement, with more potential meanings to it perhaps than Severn supposed. It might be Keats regretted that the rough world takes off the fine point of your soul, wears down something that indeed should be protected at all costs. Or it might be that Keats felt this is a good, though perhaps painful, definitely inevitable process – that one shouldn't be too precious or cling to perfection rather than be a part of the world. Should we nurture the fine point of our souls, or lose it without regret by participating in the rough and tumble of life?

Perhaps, in Keats' astute and complex mind, there was truth in both meanings, and a tension between them. If he really did feel it needed to be lost at some stage as one grew, then he needn't have called it a *fine* point, which is such a positive term. After reading *Adonais*, most of the world probably considers our friend as nothing but the fine point, and too sensitive for the world – but you and I know better than that.

I like to think that he embodied both meanings. That he lived in the tension between the exquisite and the engaged. Which was what made him so rare and wonderful a man. He kept the fine point of his soul, though it was perhaps mildly abraded. His soul was whole and true – but that did not mean he could not have lived in this world, nor written poetry and healed souls, nor practiced medicine and healed bodies, nor married you, Miss Brawne, nor raised happy children.

His last thoughts were of you, his love, his lady, his darling girl. My first thoughts likewise. I will be with you soon, Miss Brawne, and we will talk of John Keats.

I must acknowledge a debt of gratitude to some wonderful biographies:

Keats by Andrew Motion, above all;

Shelley: The Pursuit by Richard Holmes;

Being Shelley by Ann Wroe;

Byron: A Portrait by Leslie A Marchand;

Byron: The Flawed Angel by Phyllis Grosskurth; and

Mary Shelley by Miranda Seymour.

Acknowledgement is also due to *The Marriage of Cadmus and Harmony* by Roberto Calasso.

However, these fine scholars cannot be blamed for my own fancies, errors, deliberate misreadings, and detours down fictional byways.

This novel is dedicated to my sister Bryn Hammond, who encouraged, enthused and questioned in all the right measures.

She is the author of *Amgalant*, historical fiction on the Mongols and Genghis Khan. You can find her wonderful work at amgalant.com

My goal was to set this story as neatly as possible within what we know of history, so I was as true as I could be to the time and place and people. Also, it seemed vital that at the end of the story, everything was 'reset' from fancy to reality; hence Keats' death at the same time, if not quite the same place. Importantly, these characters reflect my (inevitably partial) understanding of and love for Keats, Severn, the Shelleys, Byron and Fletcher, but I tried to do them full justice.

John Keats' journey to Italy for what was to be the last four months of his life was indeed real, as was the devoted friendship of his companion Joseph Severn. Unfortunately, however, Keats' consumptive condition was already far beyond remedy. Despite a brief appearance of improvement when he first arrived in Rome, his health dwindled, and eventually he died a little before 11 o'clock on the night of 23 February 1821. He was only 25 years old. Keats was buried in the old part of the Protestant Cemetery, where we can still pay our respects today.

There was a real Lieutenant Sullivan of the British Navy who unwittingly boarded the *Maria Crowther* along with his six seamen, and was stuck in quarantine with Keats, Severn and the others. Beyond that fact, I know nothing of the historical man, and made him up out of whole cloth to suit the story. Given that he's my point-of-view character, I am sure I took many liberties. Apologies for any infelicities are offered to anyone who knows him better than I do!

Similarly, there was a real Dr James Clarke, who had charge of Keats' health in Rome. It suited my story to have him withdraw from the fray, but the historical man was as attentive to Keats during those hundred days as anyone could have asked. The medical knowledge of the day relating to consumption seems nigh on useless, but Dr Clarke did the best he could within limitations that weren't of his making.

There was also a real Reverend Mr Wolff, the English chaplain in Rome who read the service over Keats' grave. I know nothing of him other than his name, so again I invented his character to serve the story.

The Shelleys were in Italy at the time, living in Pisa, along with Mary's stepsister Claire Clairmont. Shelley's letter offering help and hospitality to

Keats, written from Italy while Keats was still in England, was real. Byron and Fletcher were also in the country, and living in Ravenna. However, none of them actually met with Keats in Rome.

My use of 'Lord C—' in the novel was intended as Sullivan's tactful avoidance of naming someone. This was a common device for potentially controversial names and places in nineteenth century novels, though the current advice seems to be that 'this quaint affectation is now dead'. I was toying with the notion that the very real Lord Castlereagh was implicated in the dastardly plot, but neither Sullivan nor I wanted to annoy the man, let alone libel him.

In the last chapter, I compressed time a little so that Sullivan could tell us something of what happened to the various characters. Here is a rather fuller version!

Percy Bysshe Shelley wrote *Adonais*, his elegy on the death of Keats, in 1821, and it has become one of his best-loved poems. Shelley drowned on 8 July 1822, aged 29. His body was washed ashore some days later, and was identified in part by the book of Keats' poetry in his pocket. He was buried in the new part of the Protestant Cemetery in Rome. There is a stone placed in the grass near the Pyramid of Cestius in the Old Cemetery to honour the Shelleys' beloved little Willmouse, but it does not mark the exact place the child was buried.

The widowed Mary Wollstonecraft Shelley returned to England with her son Percy Florence Shelley, and continued to work as a professional author. She died in London on 1 February 1851 at the age of 53, of a brain tumour. She is buried in Bournemouth, along with her son and daughter-in-law, and her parents Mary Wollstonecraft and William Godwin.

George Gordon Byron, the 6th Baron Byron, went to Greece from Italy, to serve in the cause of Greek independence from the Ottoman Empire. He died of a fever in Missolonghi on 19 April 1824, aged 36. His valet William Fletcher accompanied his remains to England, where Byron is buried in Hucknall, Nottinghamshire, near his former estate Newstead Abbey. His daughter Ada, Countess of Lovelace, a significant mathematician, is buried beside him.

William Fletcher died in 1839, in his mid-sixties, in the poorhouse – a fact I find particularly distressing.

Joseph Severn continued to live in Rome after Keats' death, working successfully as an artist. In 1828 Severn married Elizabeth Montgomerie, the illegitimate daughter of Lord Montgomerie and the ward of Lady Westmoreland, and they had several children, three of whom became artists. In 1841 they returned to England, where Severn's artistic career was less successful – but in 1861 he was appointed as British Consul in Rome. Severn died on 3 August 1879, aged 85, and in accordance with his wishes was buried next to Keats in the Protestant Cemetery.

Severn has often been accused of making the most of his association with Keats. If he did, though, I feel he earned it. No one had thought he would prove a very useful companion to Keats on this last journey, and he only seemed to be chosen because no one else was available. Severn rose to the challenge, however, and looked after Keats with loving diligence.

Frances 'Fanny' Brawne was only 20 years old when Keats died in 1821. Despite their engagement being private and informal, she went into full mourning for years, as if she were his widow. She befriended Keats' young sister, also Frances, and the two women were a great support to each other. Finally, in 1833, Fanny Brawne married Louis Lindo (later 'Lindon'), and they had three children. Nevertheless – and despite remaining discreet to the point of secrecy about her first love – Fanny wore the ring Keats gave her, and kept his books and his letters to her, for the rest of her life.

Fanny died on 4 December 1865, at the age of 65, and was buried in Brompton Cemetery, London. When her husband Louis Lindon died in 1872, he was laid to rest in the same grave. The name 'Fanny Brawne' has since been added to their shared headstone.

About Julie Bozza

I was born in England and lived most of my life in Australia before returning to the UK some years ago; my dual nationality means that I am often a bit too cheeky, but will always apologize for it.

I have been writing fiction for over thirty years, mostly for the enjoyment of myself and my friends, but writing is my love and my vocation so of course that's where my dreams and ambitions are. In the meantime, technical writing helps to pay the mortgage, while I also have fun with web design, reading, watching movies and television, knitting, and imbibing espresso.

Other titles by Julie Bozza:

The Apothecary's Garden

Butterfly Hunter

Of Dreams and Ceremonies

The Thousand Smiles of Nicholas Goring

The Definitive Albert J. Sterne

Albert J. Sterne: Future Bright, Past Imperfect

Homosapien … a fantasy about pro wrestling

Mitch Rebecki Gets a Life

A Pride of Poppies (anthology)

A Threefold Cord

The 'True Love' Solution

The Valley of the Shadow of Death

If you would like to know more, please come and join the conversation at juliebozza.com

www.ingramcontent.com/pod-product-compliance
Lightning Source LLC
Chambersburg PA
CBHW070308120726
47910CB00007B/2401